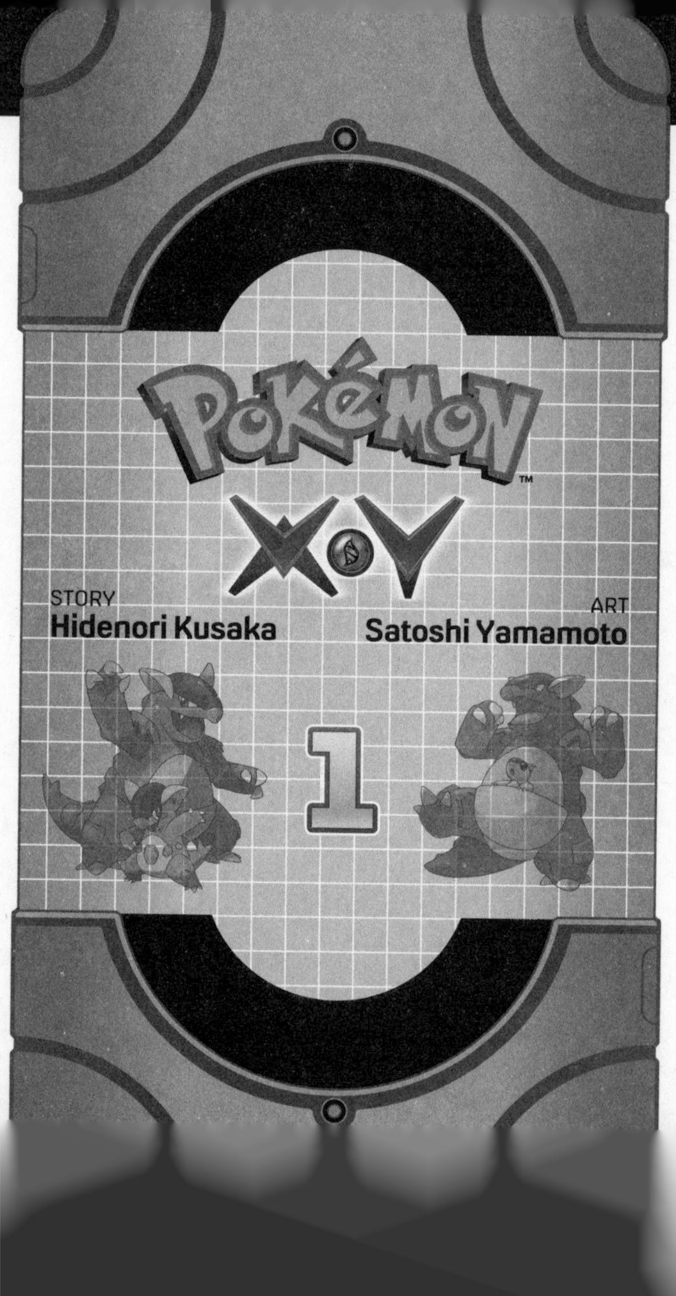
Pokémon™
X•Y
STORY
Hidenori Kusaka
ART
Satoshi Yamamoto
1

# CHARACTERS

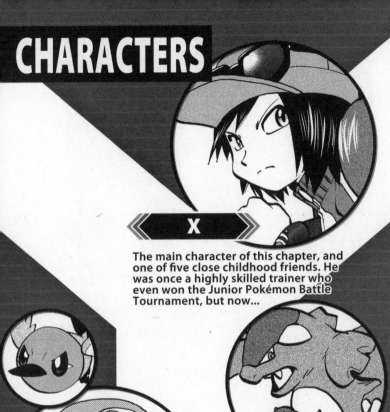

## X

The main character of this chapter, and one of five close childhood friends. He was once a highly skilled trainer who even won the Junior Pokémon Battle Tournament, but now...

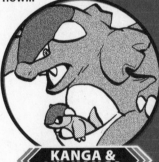

## KANGA & LI'L KANGA

X's longtime Pokémon partners with whom he won the Junior Tournament.

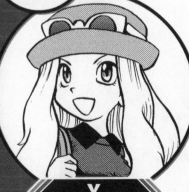

## Y

X's best friend, a Sky Trainer trainee. Her full name is Yvonne Gabena.

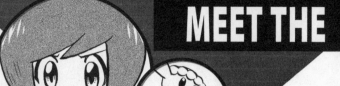

# MEET THE

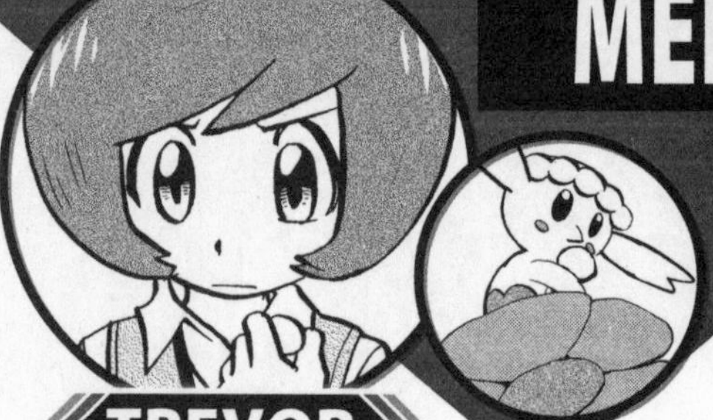

**TREVOR**

One of the five friends. A quiet boy who hopes to become a Pokémon Researcher one day.

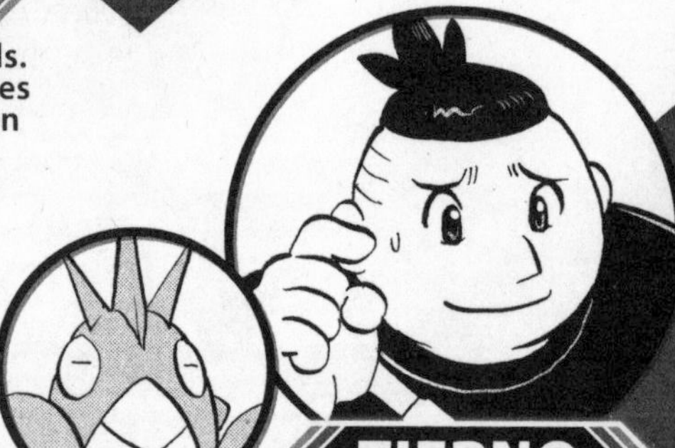

**TIERNO**

One of the five friends. A big boy with an even bigger heart. He is currently training to become a dancer.

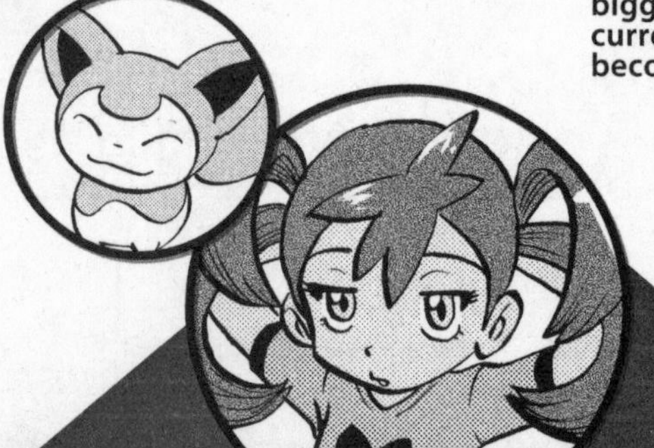

**SHAUNA**

One of the five friends. Her dream is to become a Furfrou Groomer. She is quick to speak her mind.

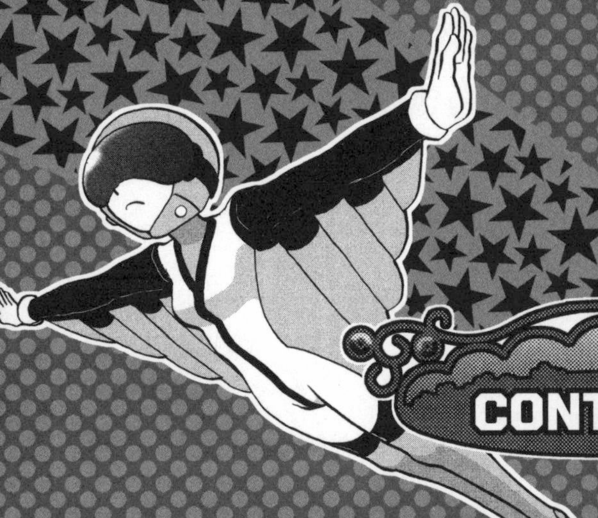

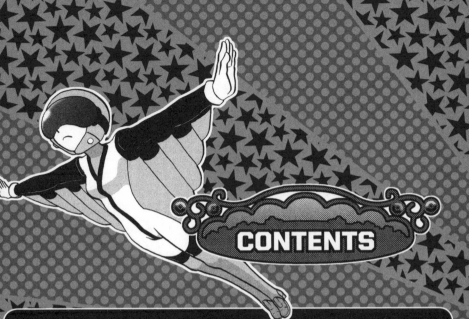

# CONTENTS



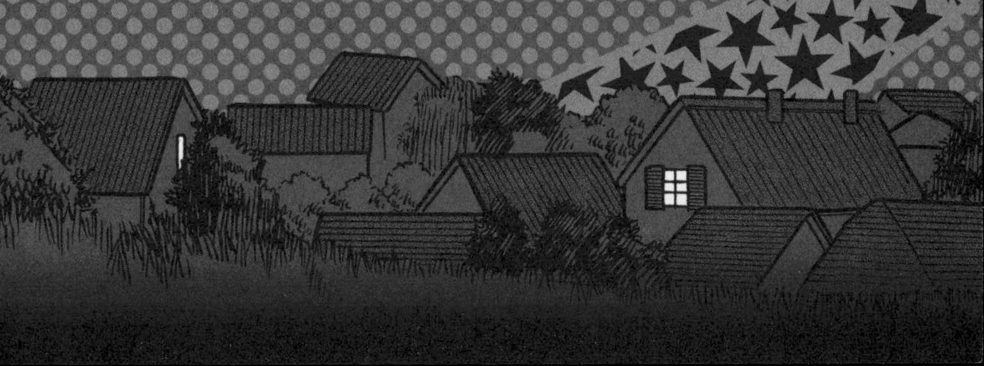

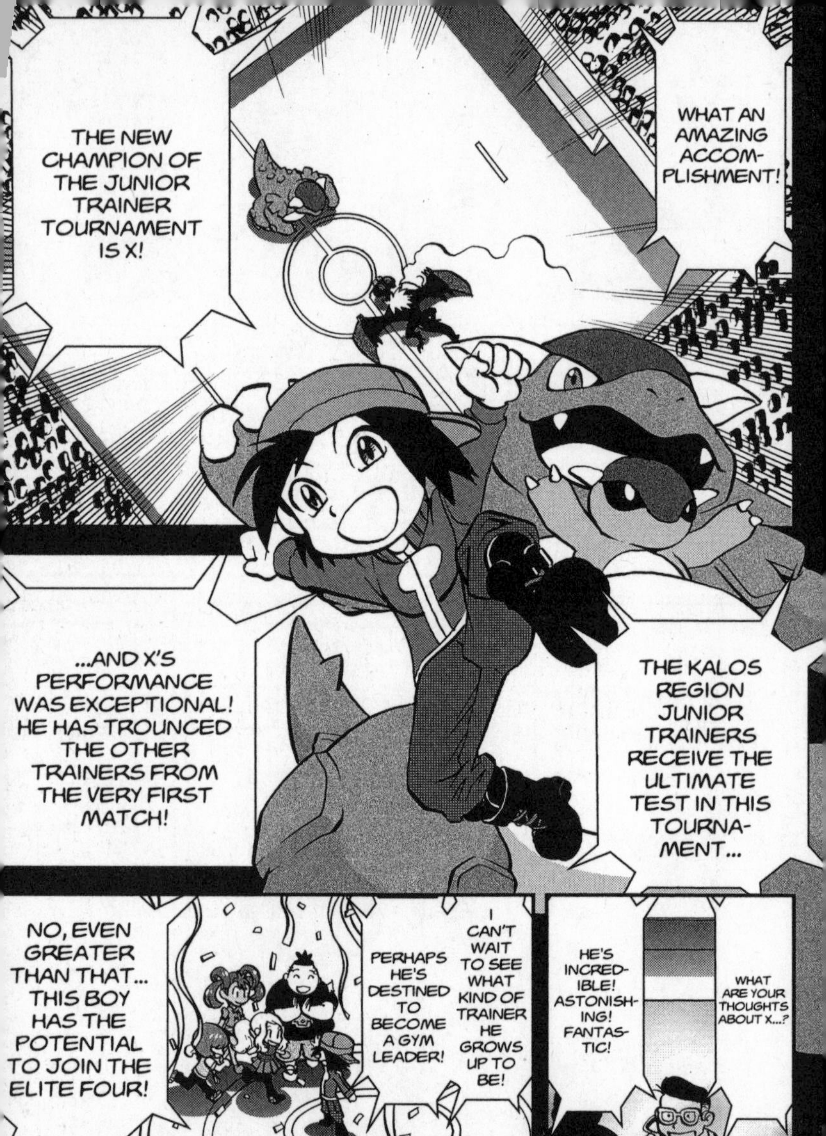
WHAT AN AMAZING ACCOM- PLISHMENT!
THE NEW CHAMPION OF THE JUNIOR TRAINER TOURNAMENT IS X!
THE KALOS REGION JUNIOR TRAINERS RECEIVE THE ULTIMATE TEST IN THIS TOURNA- MENT...
...AND X'S PERFORMANCE WAS EXCEPTIONAL! HE HAS TROUNCED THE OTHER TRAINERS FROM THE VERY FIRST MATCH!
WHAT ARE YOUR THOUGHTS ABOUT X...?
HE'S INCRED- IBLE! ASTONISH- ING! FANTAS- TIC!
I CAN'T WAIT TO SEE WHAT KIND OF TRAINER HE GROWS UP TO BE!
PERHAPS HE'S DESTINED TO BECOME A GYM LEADER!
NO, EVEN GREATER THAN THAT... THIS BOY HAS THE POTENTIAL TO JOIN THE ELITE FOUR!

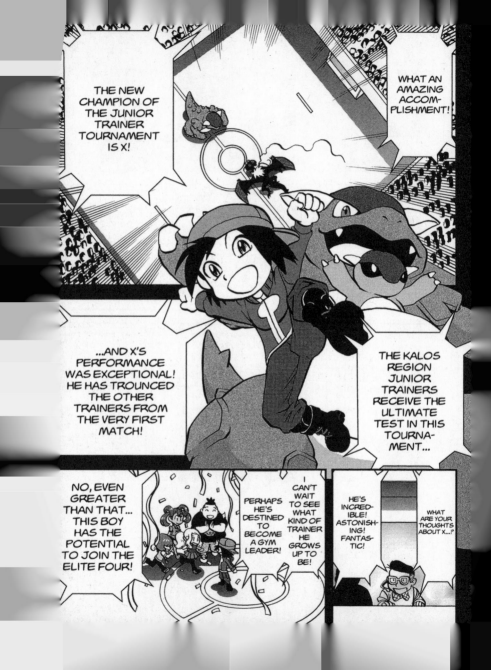

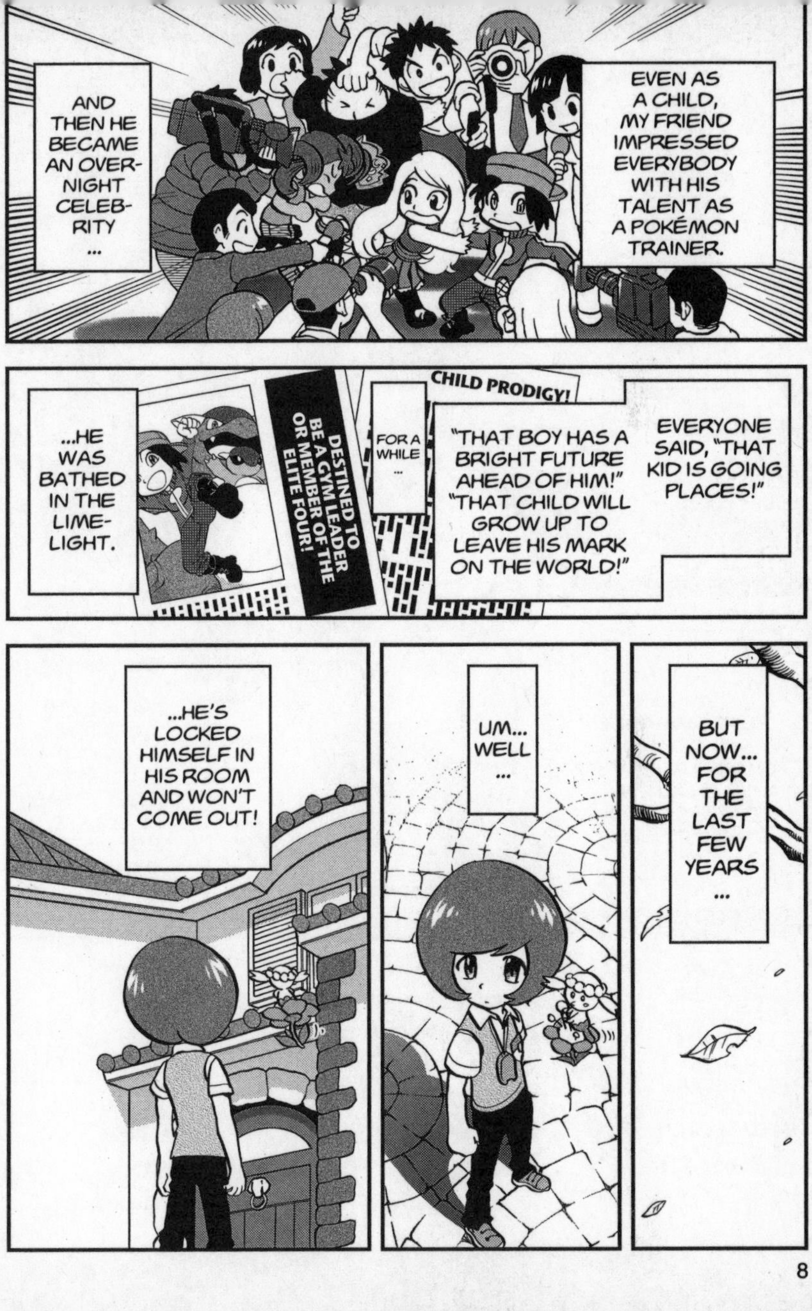
EVEN AS A CHILD, MY FRIEND IMPRESSED EVERYBODY WITH HIS TALENT AS A POKÉMON TRAINER.
AND THEN HE BECAME AN OVER-NIGHT CELEB-RITY...
CHILD PRODIGY!
EVERYONE SAID, "THAT KID IS GOING PLACES!"
"THAT BOY HAS A BRIGHT FUTURE AHEAD OF HIM!" "THAT CHILD WILL GROW UP TO LEAVE HIS MARK ON THE WORLD!"
FOR A WHILE...
DESTINED TO BE A GYM LEADER OR MEMBER OF THE ELITE FOUR!
...HE WAS BATHED IN THE LIME-LIGHT.
BUT NOW... FOR THE LAST FEW YEARS...
UM... WELL...
...HE'S LOCKED HIMSELF IN HIS ROOM AND WON'T COME OUT!

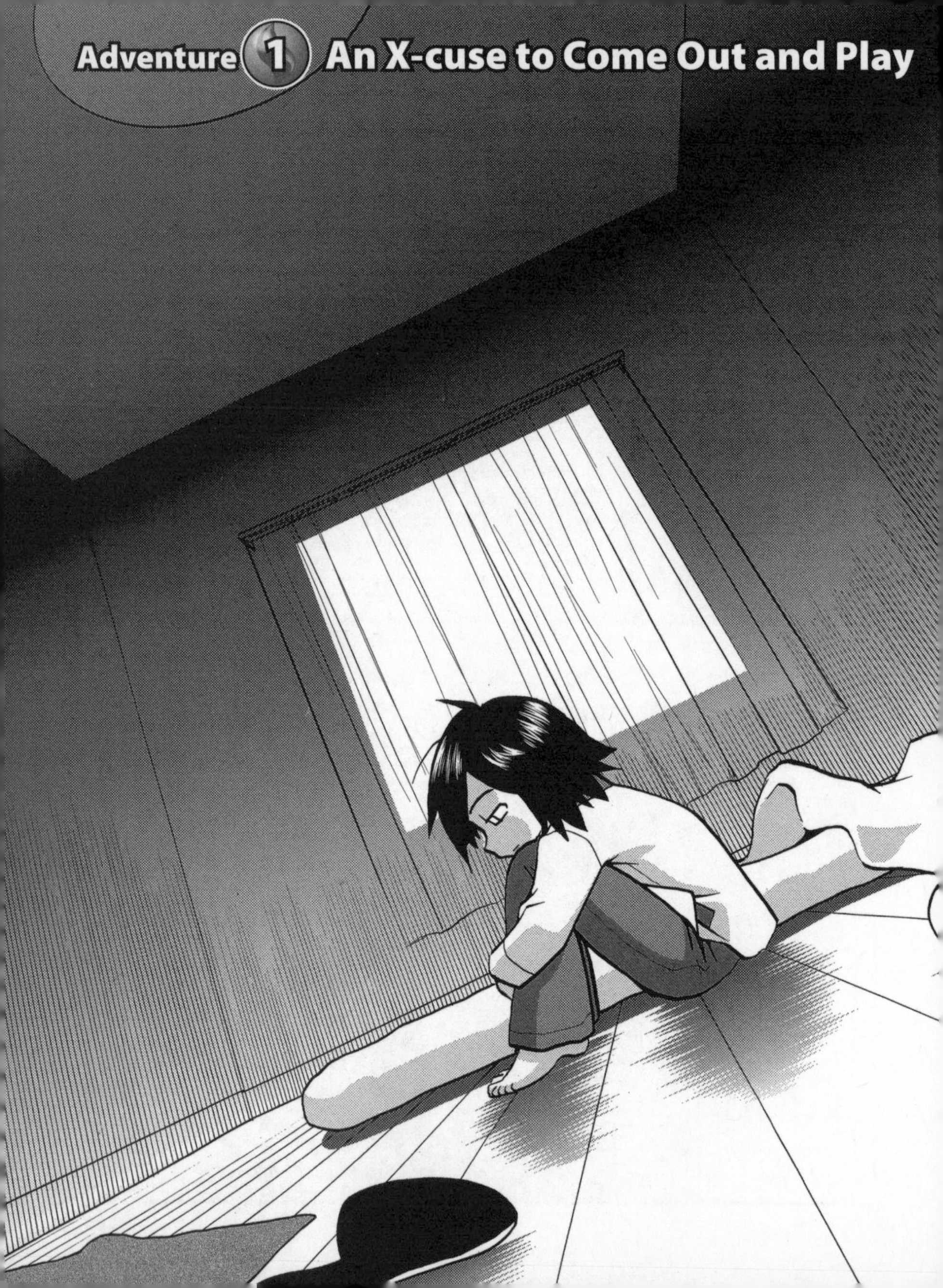
Adventure 1 An X-cuse to Come Out and Play

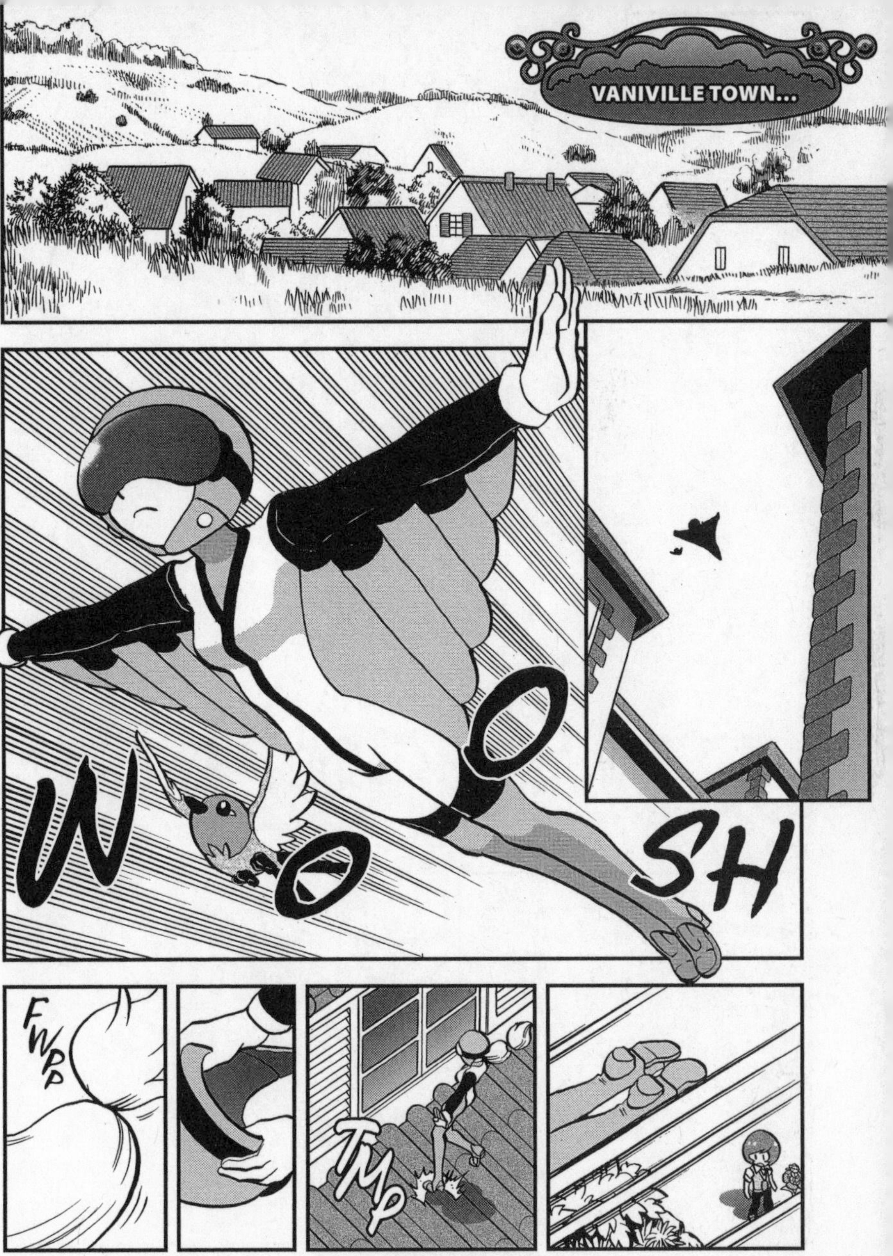
VANIVILLE TOWN...
WOOSH
TMP
FWPP

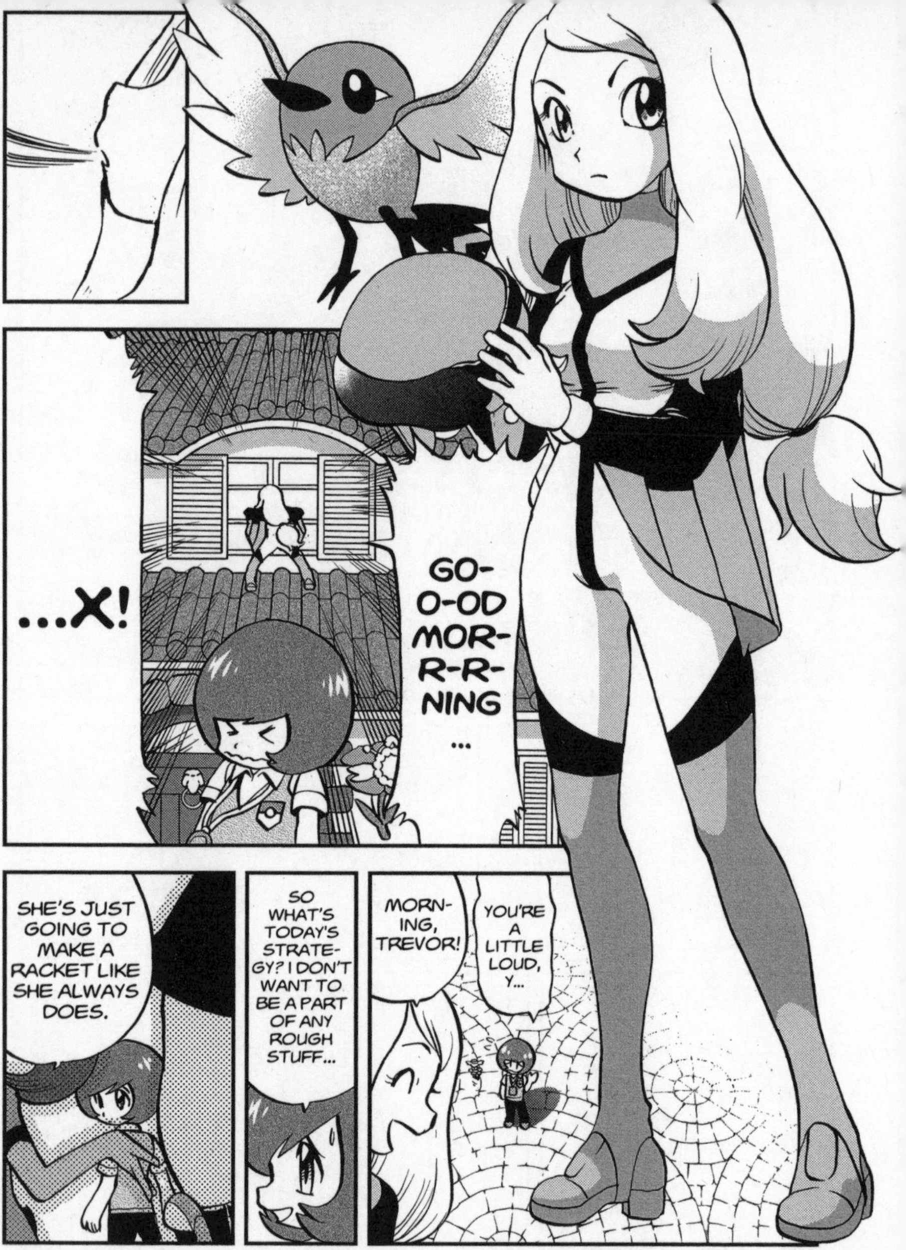
GO-O-OD MOR-R-R-NING ...
...X!
YOU'RE A LITTLE LOUD, Y...
MORNING, TREVOR!
SO WHAT'S TODAY'S STRATEGY? I DON'T WANT TO BE A PART OF ANY ROUGH STUFF...
SHE'S JUST GOING TO MAKE A RACKET LIKE SHE ALWAYS DOES.

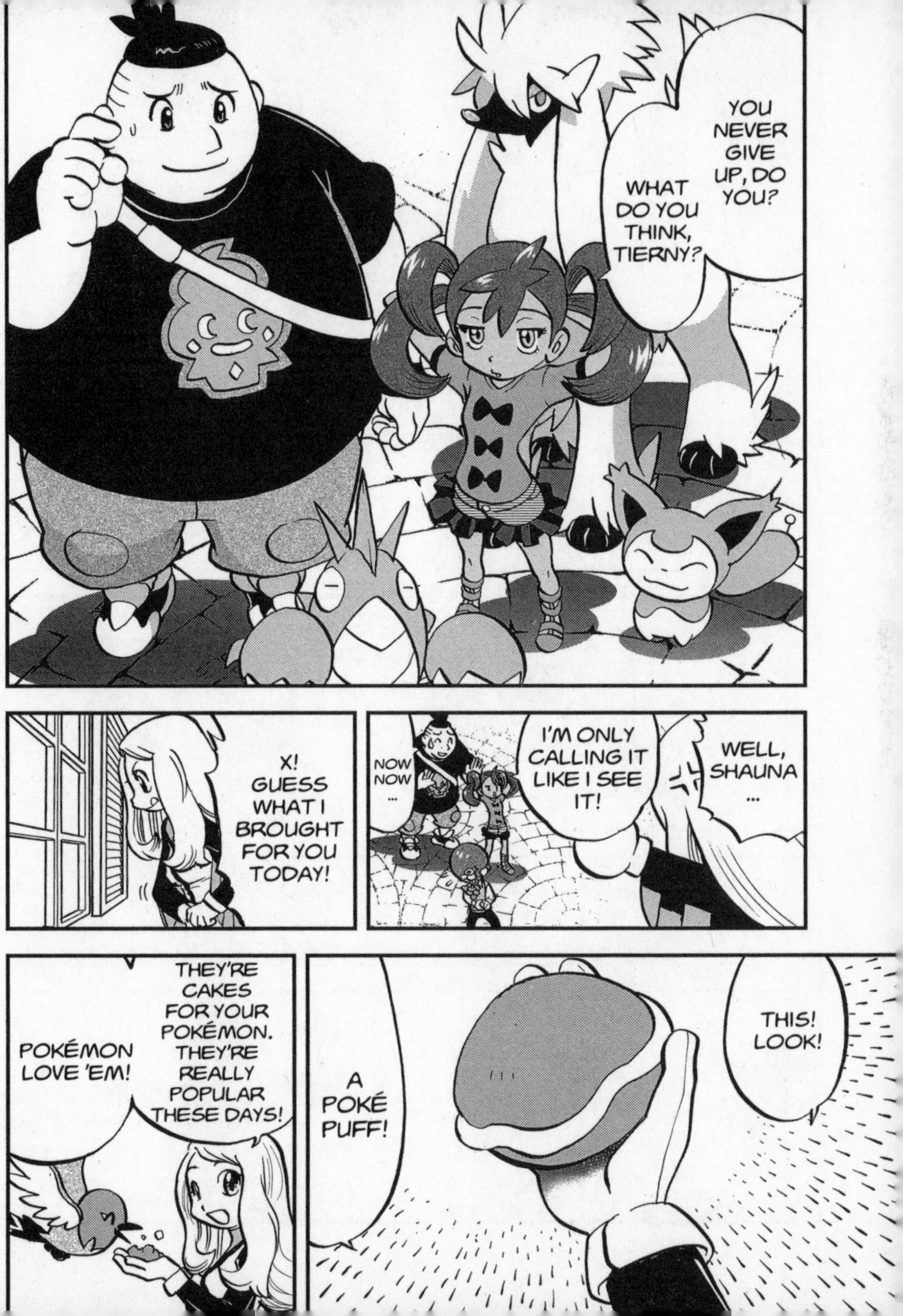
YOU NEVER GIVE UP, DO YOU?
WHAT DO YOU THINK, TIERNY?
WELL, SHAUNA ...
I'M ONLY CALLING IT LIKE I SEE IT!
NOW NOW ...
X! GUESS WHAT I BROUGHT FOR YOU TODAY!
THIS! LOOK!
A POKÉ PUFF!
THEY'RE CAKES FOR YOUR POKÉMON. THEY'RE REALLY POPULAR THESE DAYS!
POKÉMON LOVE 'EM!

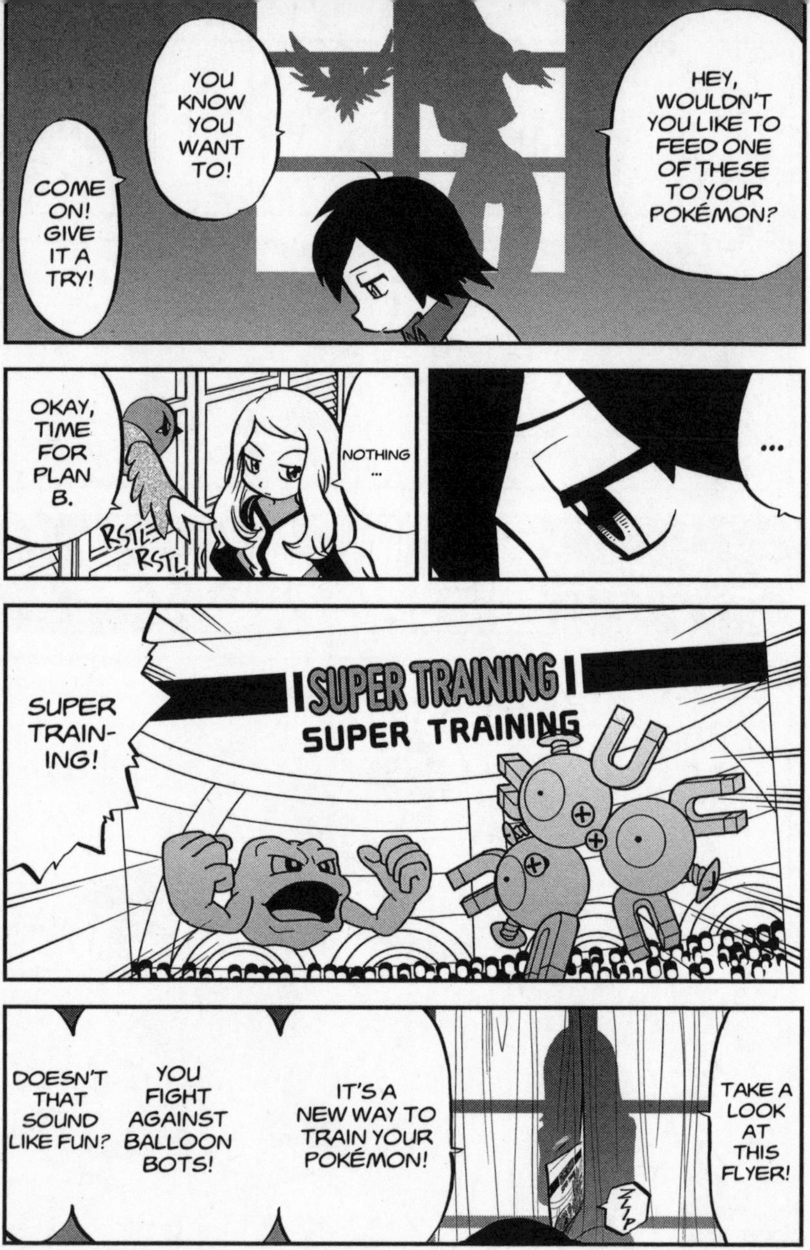
HEY, WOULDN'T YOU LIKE TO FEED ONE OF THESE TO YOUR POKÉMON?
YOU KNOW YOU WANT TO!
COME ON! GIVE IT A TRY!
...
NOTHING ...
OKAY, TIME FOR PLAN B.
RSTL RSTL
SUPER TRAINING
SUPER TRAINING
SUPER TRAIN-ING!
TAKE A LOOK AT THIS FLYER!
ZZIP
IT'S A NEW WAY TO TRAIN YOUR POKÉMON!
YOU FIGHT AGAINST BALLOON BOTS!
DOESN'T THAT SOUND LIKE FUN?

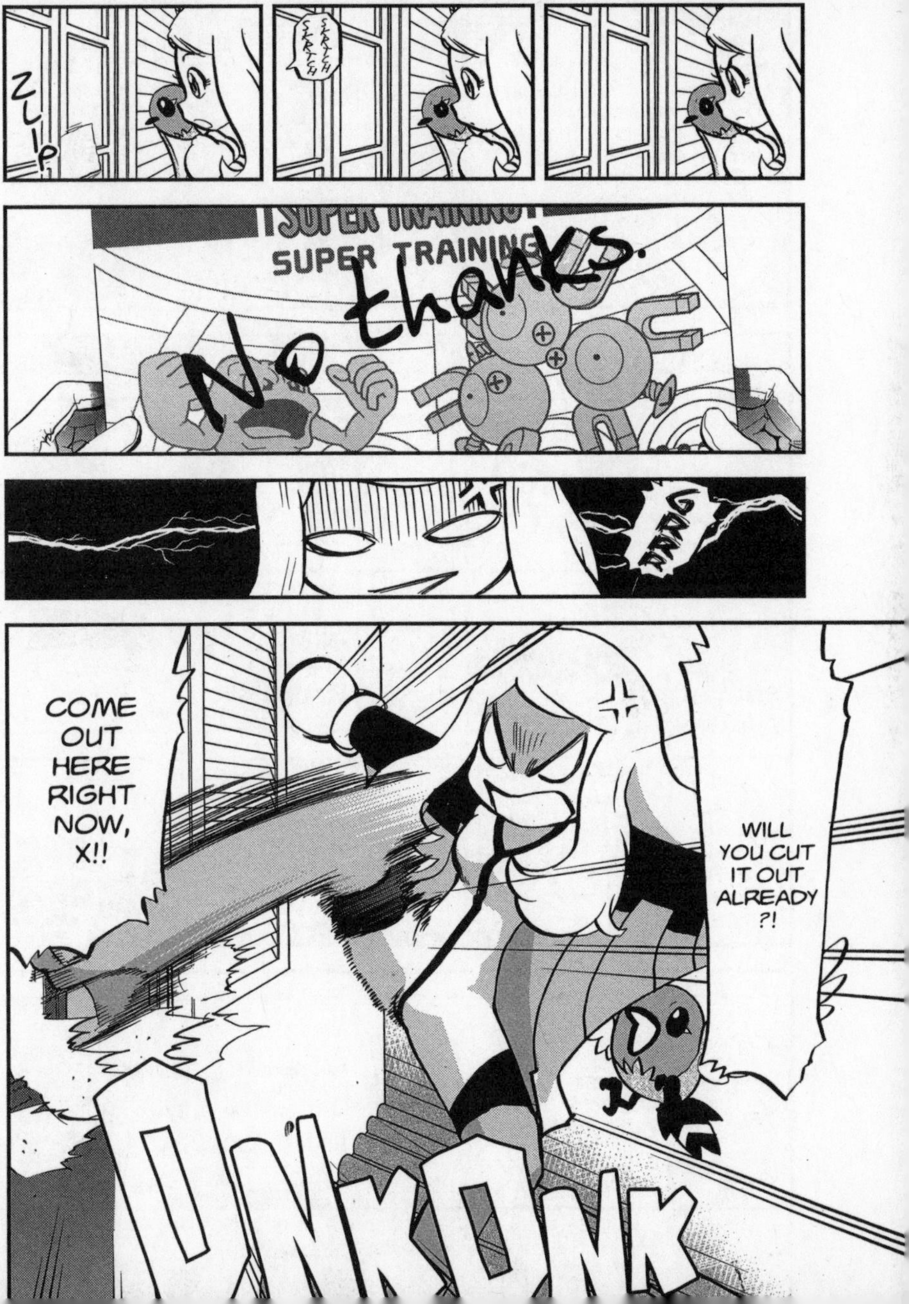
SCRATCH SCRATCH
ZLIIP
SUPER TRAINING!
SUPER TRAINING
No thanks.
GRRR
WILL YOU CUT IT OUT ALREADY?!
COME OUT HERE RIGHT NOW, X!!
ONKONK

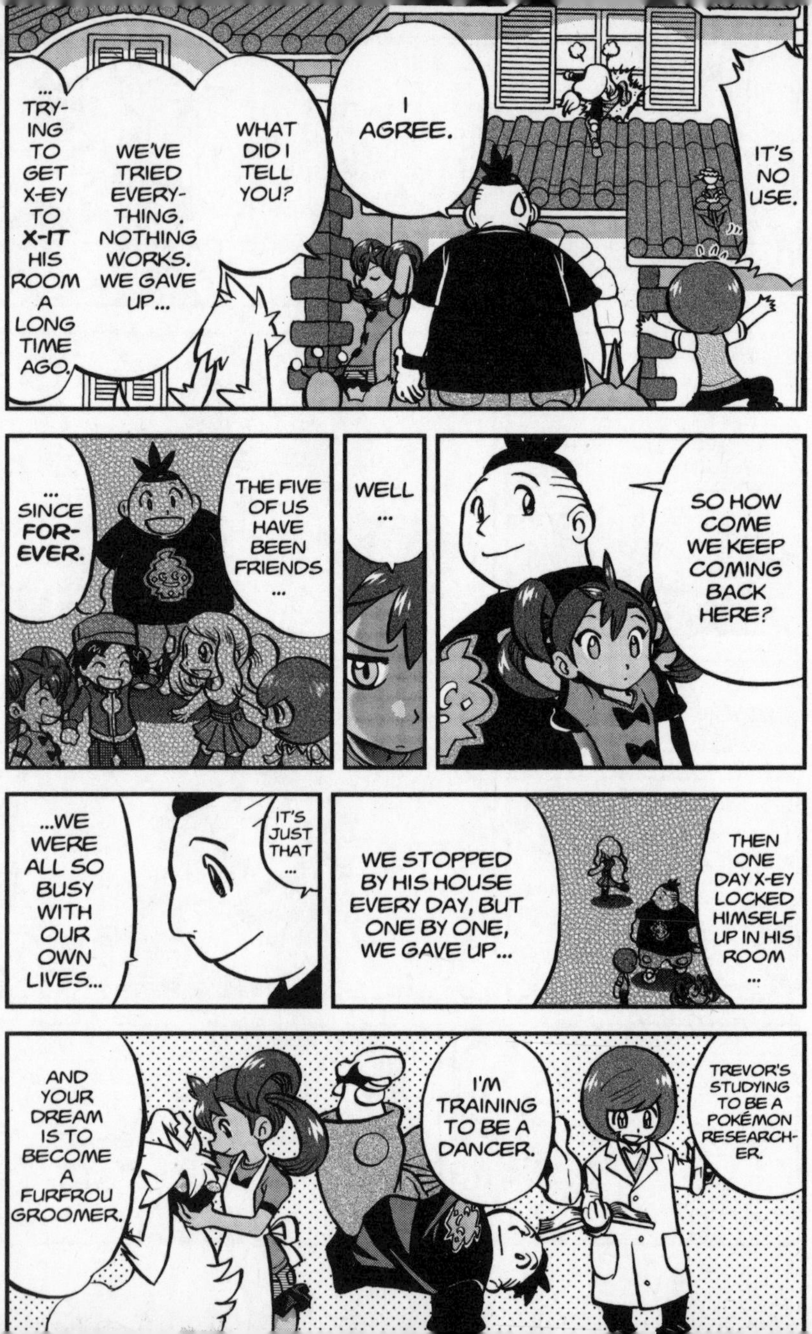
IT'S NO USE.
I AGREE.
WHAT DID I TELL YOU?
WE'VE TRIED EVERYTHING. NOTHING WORKS. WE GAVE UP...
...TRYING TO GET X-EY TO **X-IT** HIS ROOM A LONG TIME AGO.
SO HOW COME WE KEEP COMING BACK HERE?
WELL...
THE FIVE OF US HAVE BEEN FRIENDS...
...SINCE **FOREVER.**
THEN ONE DAY X-EY LOCKED HIMSELF UP IN HIS ROOM...
WE STOPPED BY HIS HOUSE EVERY DAY, BUT ONE BY ONE, WE GAVE UP...
IT'S JUST THAT...
...WE WERE ALL SO BUSY WITH OUR OWN LIVES...
TREVOR'S STUDYING TO BE A POKÉMON RESEARCHER.
I'M TRAINING TO BE A DANCER.
AND YOUR DREAM IS TO BECOME A FURFROU GROOMER.

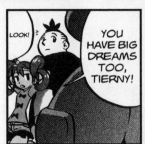

LOOK!

YOU HAVE BIG DREAMS TOO, TIERNY!

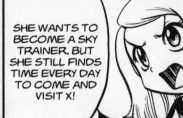

SHE WANTS TO BECOME A SKY TRAINER. BUT SHE STILL FINDS TIME EVERY DAY TO COME AND VISIT X!

Y HAS **REALLY** BIG DREAMS.

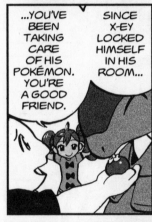

...YOU'VE BEEN TAKING CARE OF HIS POKÉMON. YOU'RE A GOOD FRIEND.

SINCE X-EY LOCKED HIMSELF IN HIS ROOM...

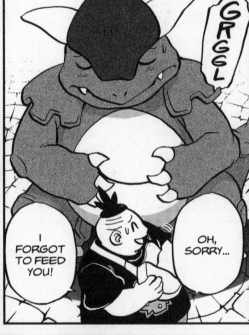

GRGGL

I FORGOT TO FEED YOU!

OH, SORRY...

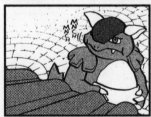

MNCH

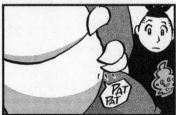

PAT PAT

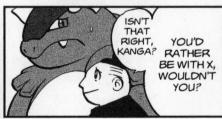

ISN'T THAT RIGHT, KANGA?

YOU'D RATHER BE WITH X, WOULDN'T YOU?

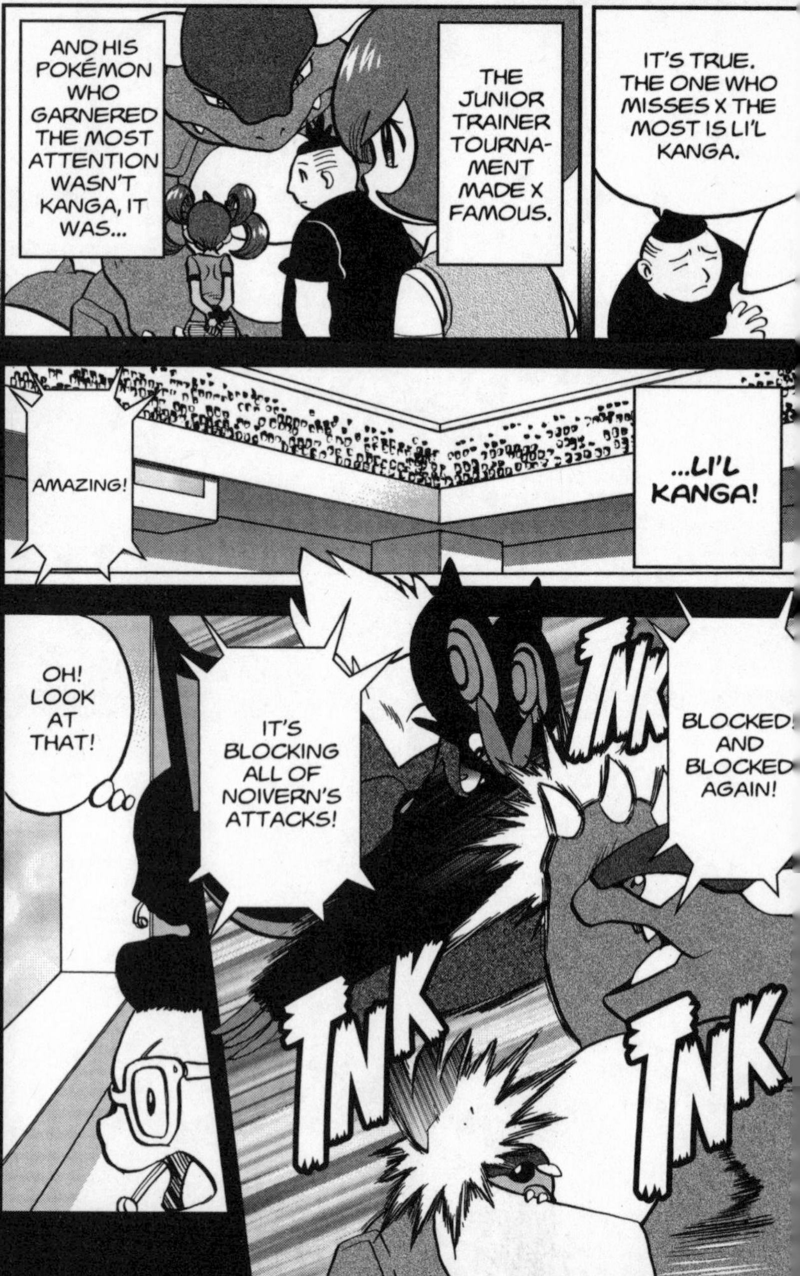
IT'S TRUE. THE ONE WHO MISSES X THE MOST IS LI'L KANGA.
THE JUNIOR TRAINER TOURNAMENT MADE X FAMOUS.
AND HIS POKÉMON WHO GARNERED THE MOST ATTENTION WASN'T KANGA, IT WAS...
...LI'L KANGA!
AMAZING!
TNK
BLOCKED AND BLOCKED AGAIN!
IT'S BLOCKING ALL OF NOIVERN'S ATTACKS!
OH! LOOK AT THAT!
TNK
TNK

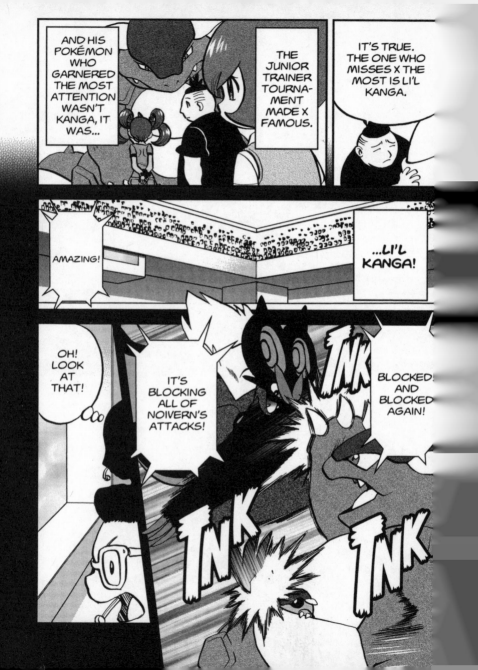

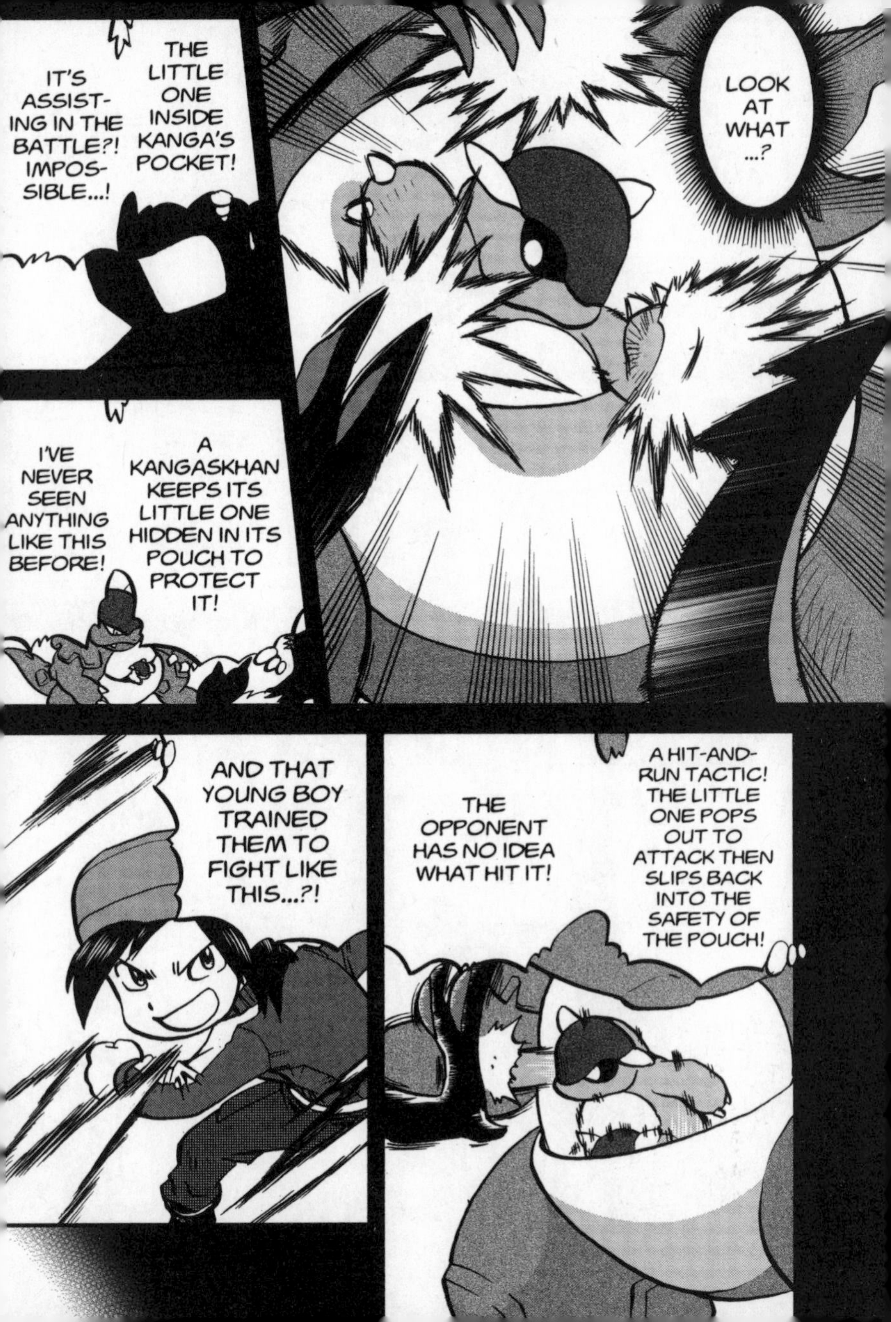
LOOK AT WHAT ...?
THE LITTLE ONE INSIDE KANGA'S POCKET!
IT'S ASSISTING IN THE BATTLE?! IMPOSSIBLE...!
A KANGASKHAN KEEPS ITS LITTLE ONE HIDDEN IN ITS POUCH TO PROTECT IT!
I'VE NEVER SEEN ANYTHING LIKE THIS BEFORE!
A HIT-AND-RUN TACTIC! THE LITTLE ONE POPS OUT TO ATTACK THEN SLIPS BACK INTO THE SAFETY OF THE POUCH!
THE OPPONENT HAS NO IDEA WHAT HIT IT!
AND THAT YOUNG BOY TRAINED THEM TO FIGHT LIKE THIS...?!

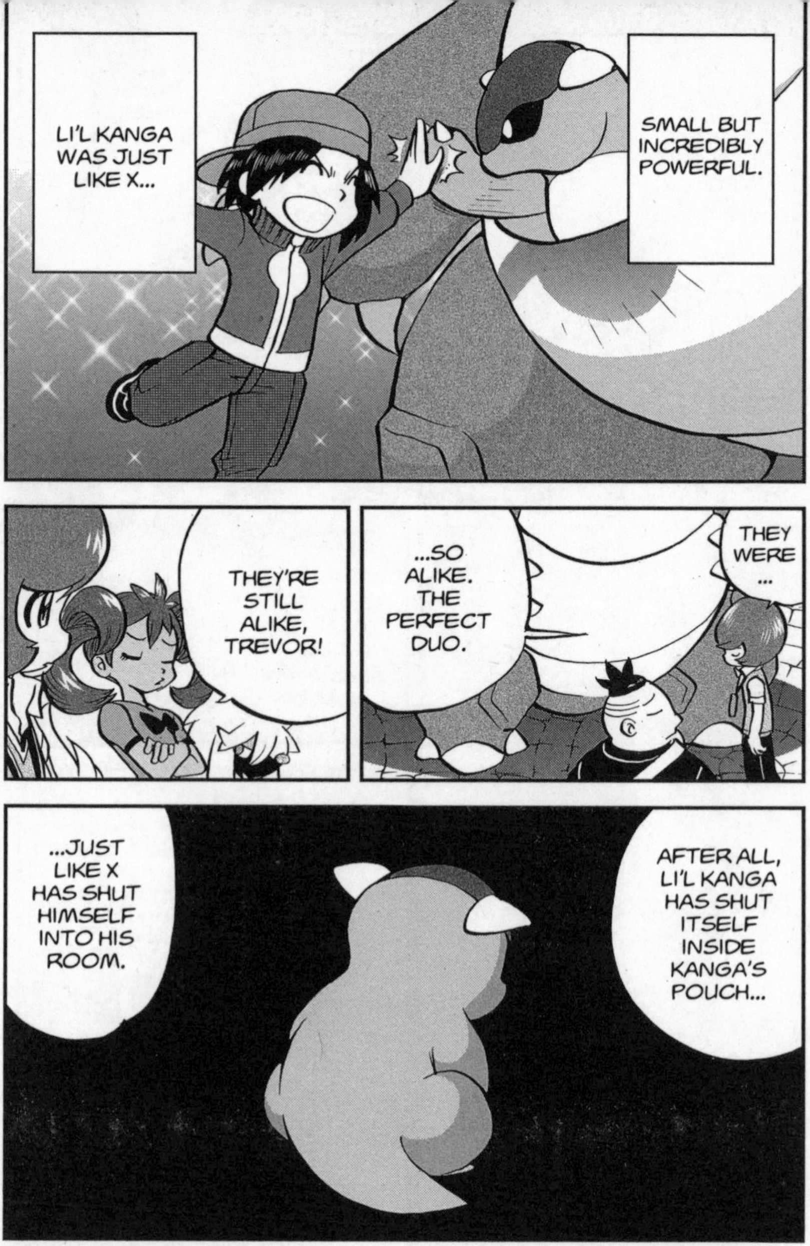
SMALL BUT INCREDIBLY POWERFUL.
LI'L KANGA WAS JUST LIKE X...
THEY WERE...
...SO ALIKE. THE PERFECT DUO.
THEY'RE STILL ALIKE, TREVOR!
AFTER ALL, LI'L KANGA HAS SHUT ITSELF INSIDE KANGA'S POUCH...
...JUST LIKE X HAS SHUT HIMSELF INTO HIS ROOM.

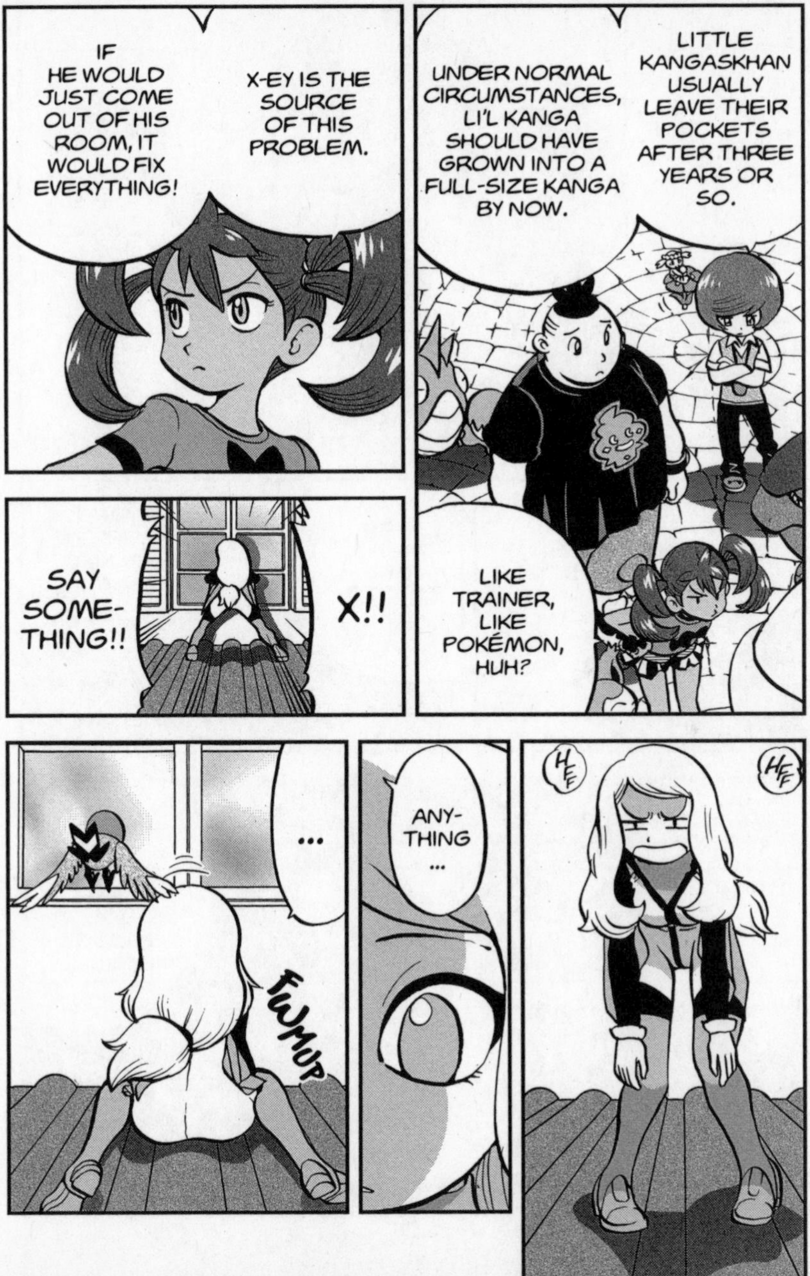
LITTLE KANGASKHAN USUALLY LEAVE THEIR POCKETS AFTER THREE YEARS OR SO.
UNDER NORMAL CIRCUMSTANCES, LI'L KANGA SHOULD HAVE GROWN INTO A FULL-SIZE KANGA BY NOW.
LIKE TRAINER, LIKE POKÉMON, HUH?
X-EY IS THE SOURCE OF THIS PROBLEM.
IF HE WOULD JUST COME OUT OF HIS ROOM, IT WOULD FIX EVERYTHING!
X!!
SAY SOME- THING!!
HFF
HFF
ANY- THING ...
...
FWUMP

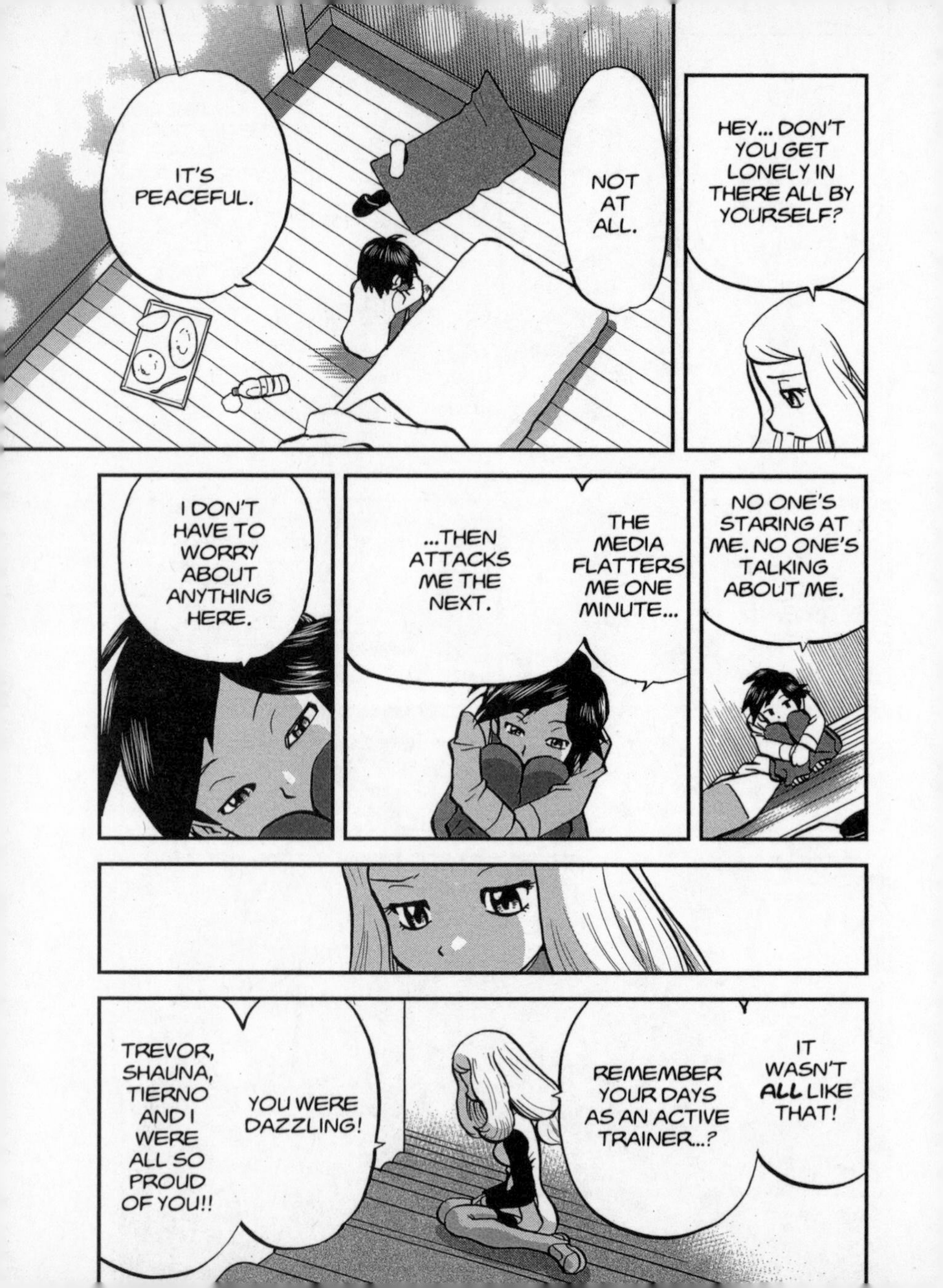
HEY... DON'T YOU GET LONELY IN THERE ALL BY YOURSELF?
NOT AT ALL.
IT'S PEACEFUL.
NO ONE'S STARING AT ME. NO ONE'S TALKING ABOUT ME.
THE MEDIA FLATTERS ME ONE MINUTE...
...THEN ATTACKS ME THE NEXT.
I DON'T HAVE TO WORRY ABOUT ANYTHING HERE.
IT WASN'T **ALL** LIKE THAT!
REMEMBER YOUR DAYS AS AN ACTIVE TRAINER...?
YOU WERE DAZZLING!
TREVOR, SHAUNA, TIERNO AND I WERE ALL SO PROUD OF YOU!!

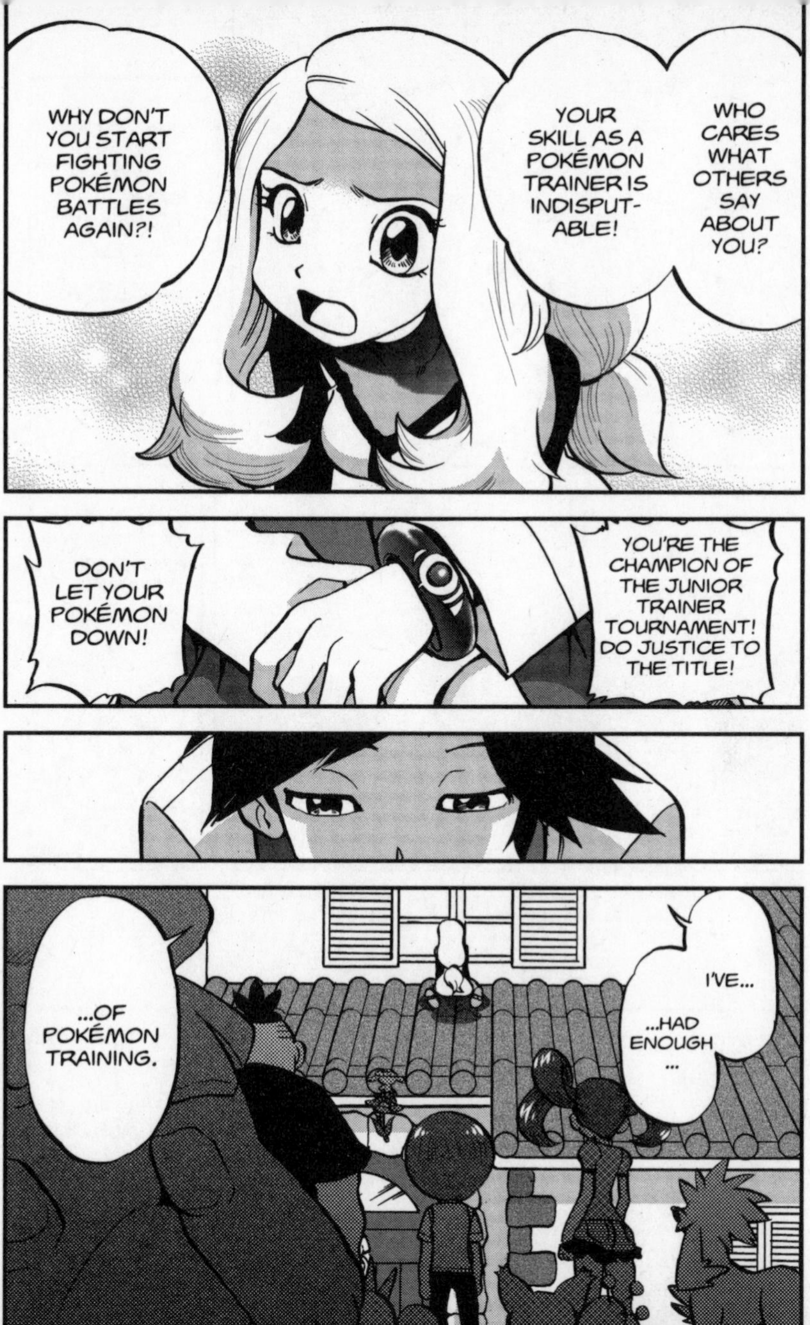
WHO CARES WHAT OTHERS SAY ABOUT YOU?
YOUR SKILL AS A POKÉMON TRAINER IS INDISPUT-ABLE!
WHY DON'T YOU START FIGHTING POKÉMON BATTLES AGAIN?!
YOU'RE THE CHAMPION OF THE JUNIOR TRAINER TOURNAMENT! DO JUSTICE TO THE TITLE!
DON'T LET YOUR POKÉMON DOWN!
I'VE...
...HAD ENOUGH ...
...OF POKÉMON TRAINING.

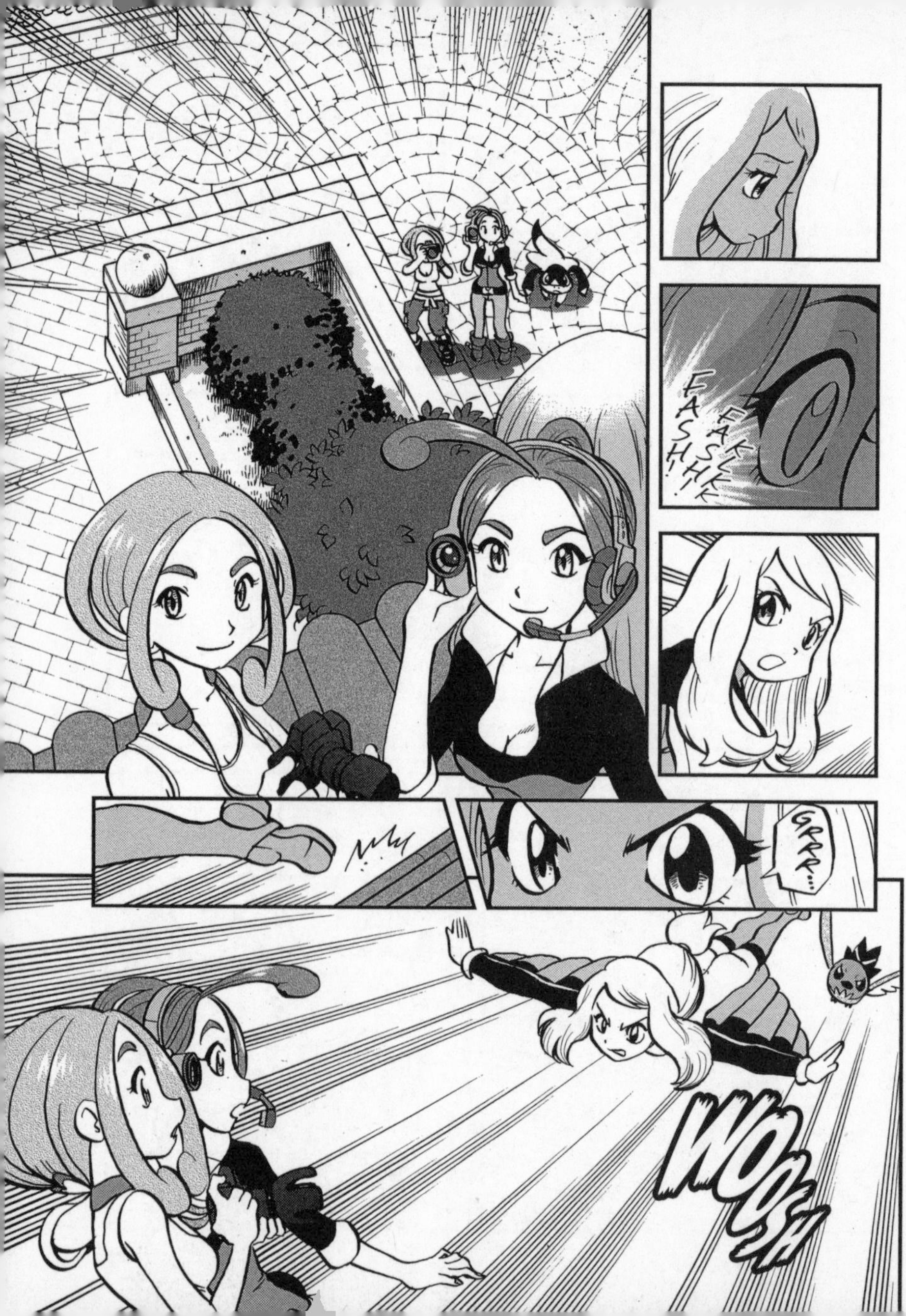
FASH!
GRRR...
WOOSH

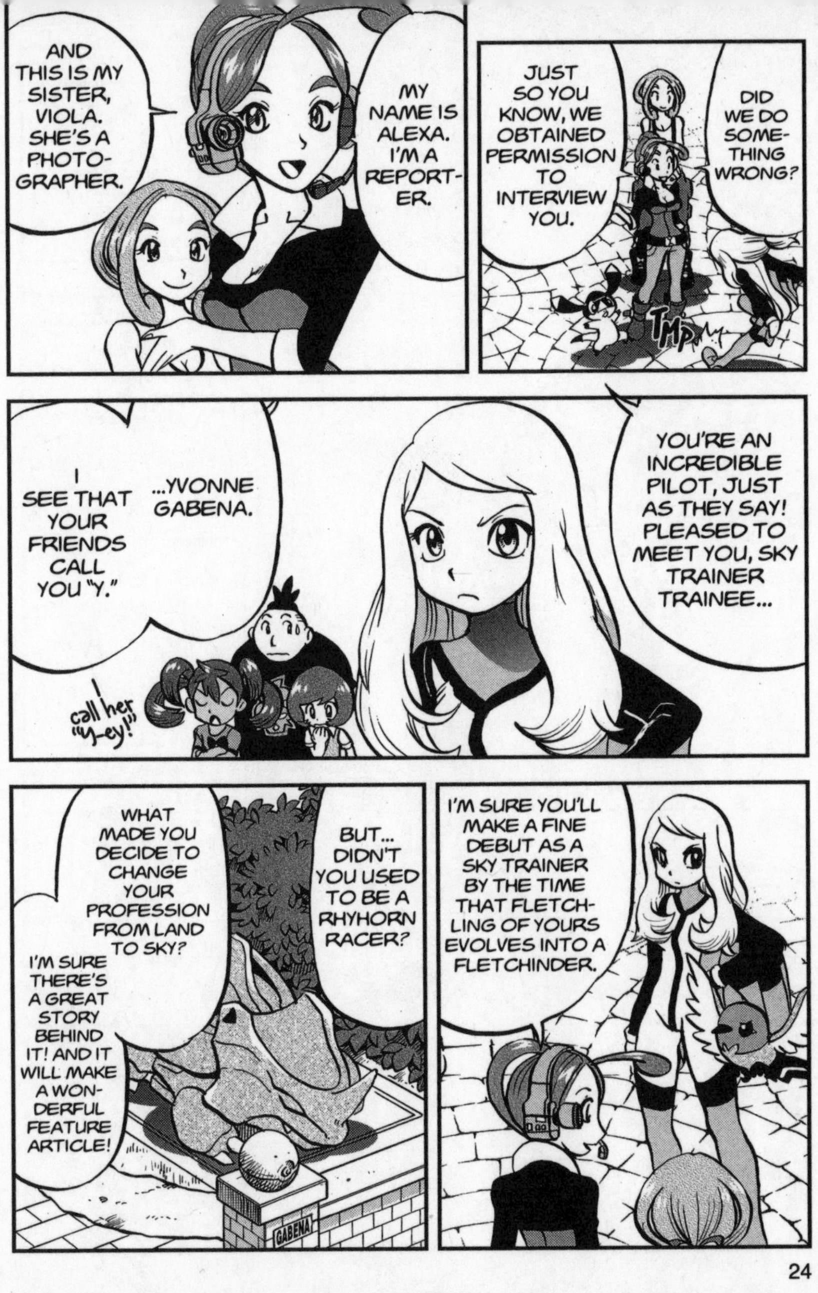
DID WE DO SOMETHING WRONG?
JUST SO YOU KNOW, WE OBTAINED PERMISSION TO INTERVIEW YOU.
TMP
MY NAME IS ALEXA. I'M A REPORTER.
AND THIS IS MY SISTER, VIOLA. SHE'S A PHOTOGRAPHER.
YOU'RE AN INCREDIBLE PILOT, JUST AS THEY SAY! PLEASED TO MEET YOU, SKY TRAINER TRAINEE...
...YVONNE GABENA.
I SEE THAT YOUR FRIENDS CALL YOU "Y."
I call her "Y-ey!"
I'M SURE YOU'LL MAKE A FINE DEBUT AS A SKY TRAINER BY THE TIME THAT FLETCHLING OF YOURS EVOLVES INTO A FLETCHINDER.
BUT... DIDN'T YOU USED TO BE A RHYHORN RACER?
WHAT MADE YOU DECIDE TO CHANGE YOUR PROFESSION FROM LAND TO SKY?
I'M SURE THERE'S A GREAT STORY BEHIND IT! AND IT WILL MAKE A WONDERFUL FEATURE ARTICLE!
GABENA

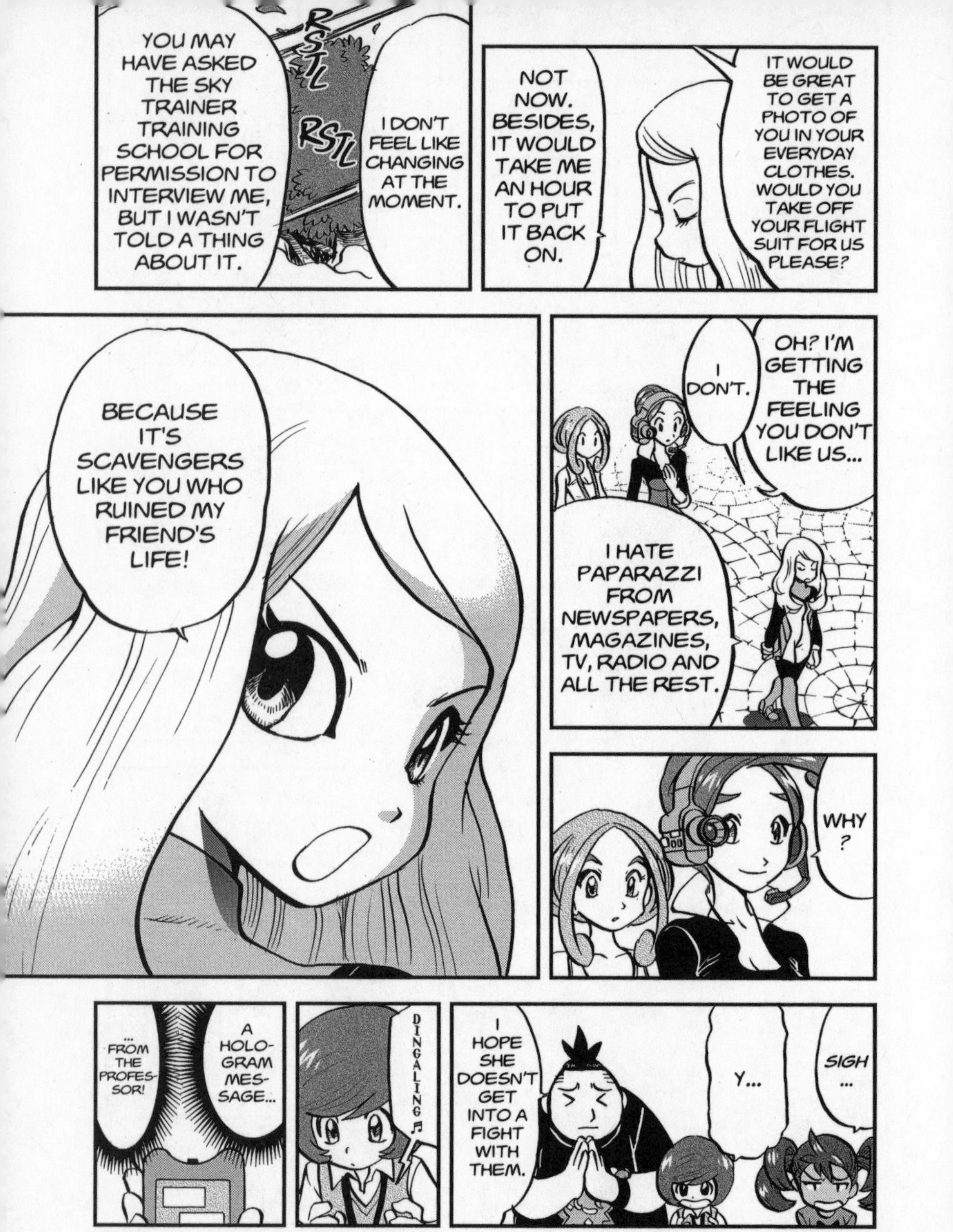
IT WOULD BE GREAT TO GET A PHOTO OF YOU IN YOUR EVERYDAY CLOTHES. WOULD YOU TAKE OFF YOUR FLIGHT SUIT FOR US PLEASE?
NOT NOW. BESIDES, IT WOULD TAKE ME AN HOUR TO PUT IT BACK ON.
I DON'T FEEL LIKE CHANGING AT THE MOMENT.
RSTL
RSTL
YOU MAY HAVE ASKED THE SKY TRAINER TRAINING SCHOOL FOR PERMISSION TO INTERVIEW ME, BUT I WASN'T TOLD A THING ABOUT IT.
OH? I'M GETTING THE FEELING YOU DON'T LIKE US...
I DON'T.
I HATE PAPARAZZI FROM NEWSPAPERS, MAGAZINES, TV, RADIO AND ALL THE REST.
WHY?
BECAUSE IT'S SCAVENGERS LIKE YOU WHO RUINED MY FRIEND'S LIFE!
SIGH...
Y...
I HOPE SHE DOESN'T GET INTO A FIGHT WITH THEM.
DINGALING ♬
A HOLOGRAM MESSAGE...
...FROM THE PROFESSOR!

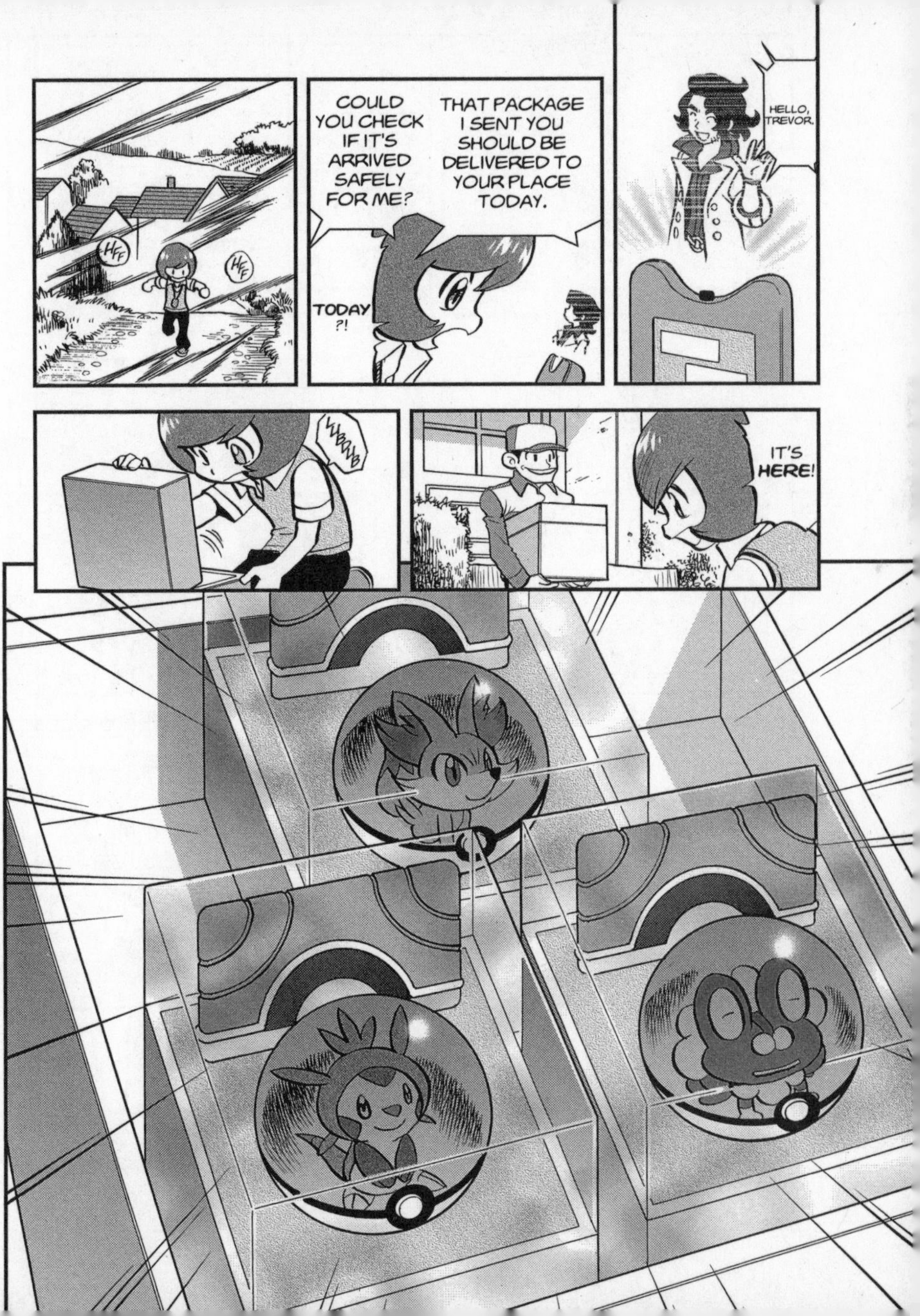
HELLO, TREVOR.
THAT PACKAGE I SENT YOU SHOULD BE DELIVERED TO YOUR PLACE TODAY.
COULD YOU CHECK IF IT'S ARRIVED SAFELY FOR ME?
TODAY?!
HFF
HFF
IT'S HERE!
LUBDUB

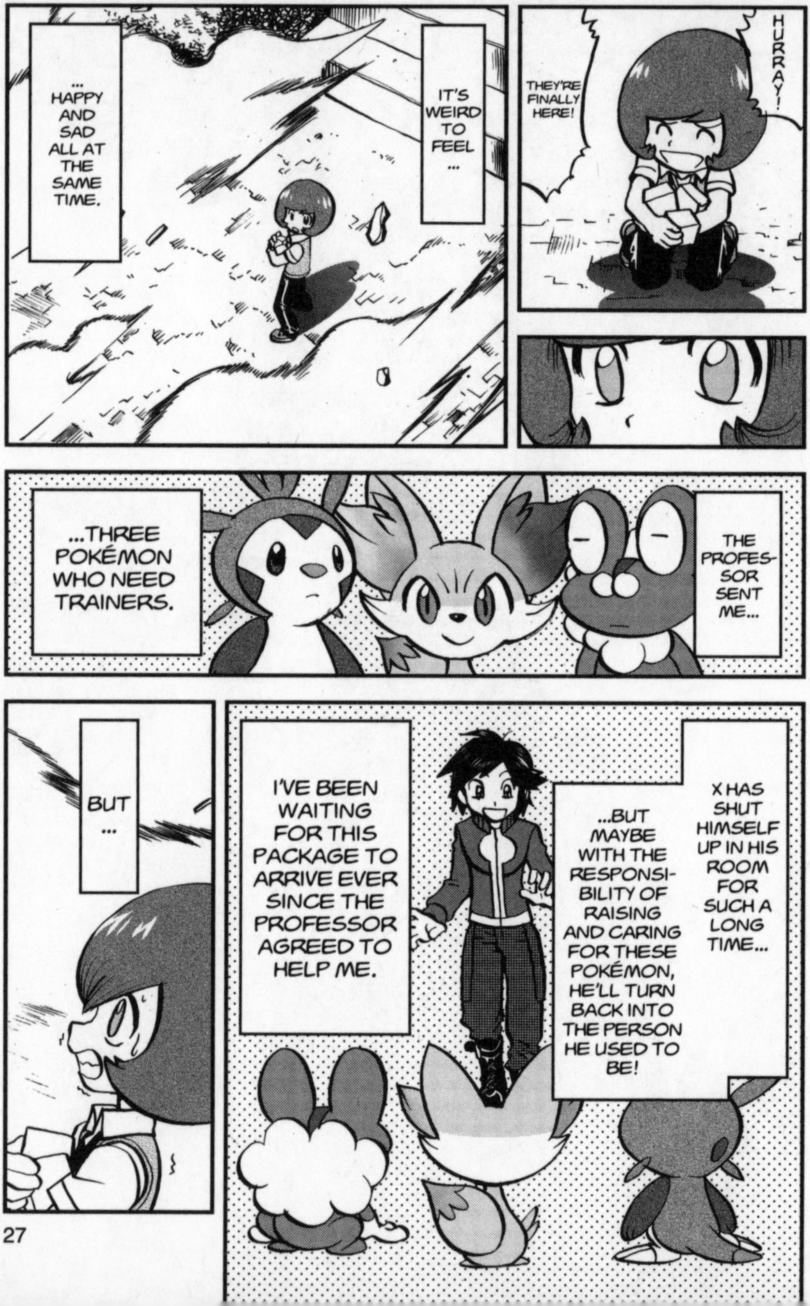
HURRAY!
THEY'RE FINALLY HERE!
IT'S WEIRD TO FEEL ...
... HAPPY AND SAD ALL AT THE SAME TIME.
THE PROFESSOR SENT ME...
...THREE POKÉMON WHO NEED TRAINERS.
X HAS SHUT HIMSELF UP IN HIS ROOM FOR SUCH A LONG TIME...
...BUT MAYBE WITH THE RESPONSIBILITY OF RAISING AND CARING FOR THESE POKÉMON, HE'LL TURN BACK INTO THE PERSON HE USED TO BE!
I'VE BEEN WAITING FOR THIS PACKAGE TO ARRIVE EVER SINCE THE PROFESSOR AGREED TO HELP ME.
BUT ...

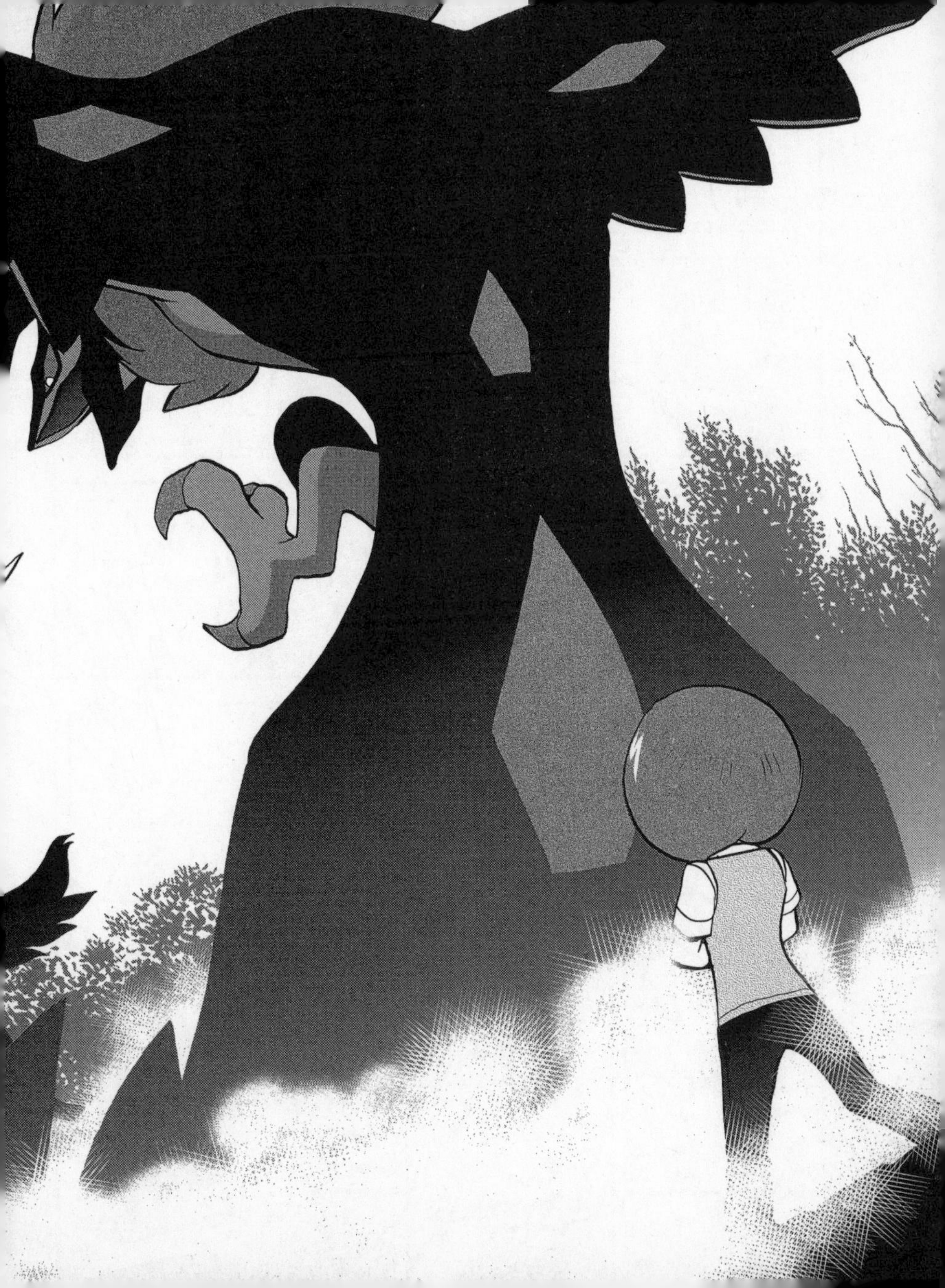

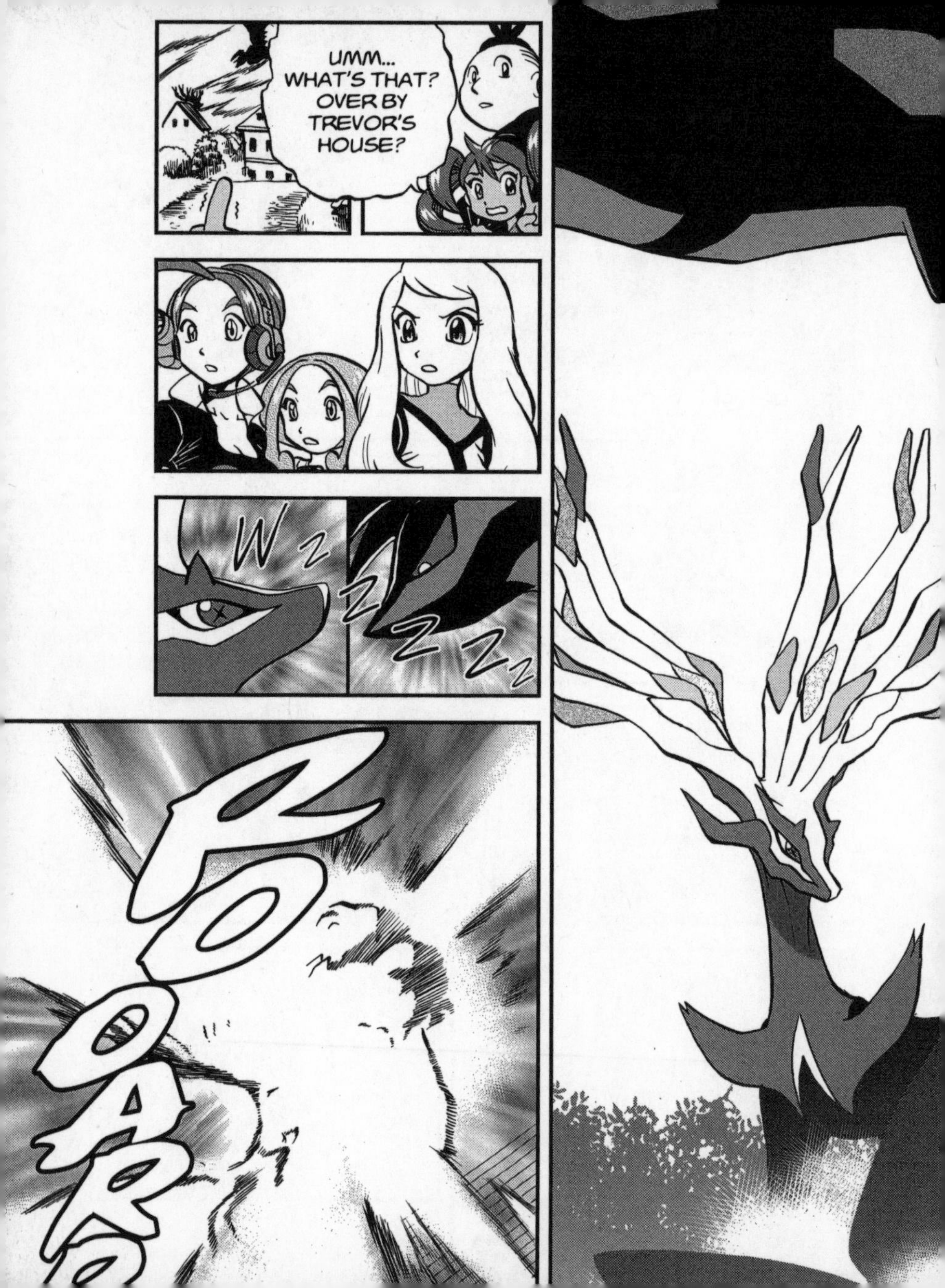
UMM... WHAT'S THAT? OVER BY TREVOR'S HOUSE?
WZZZZZZ
ROOARR

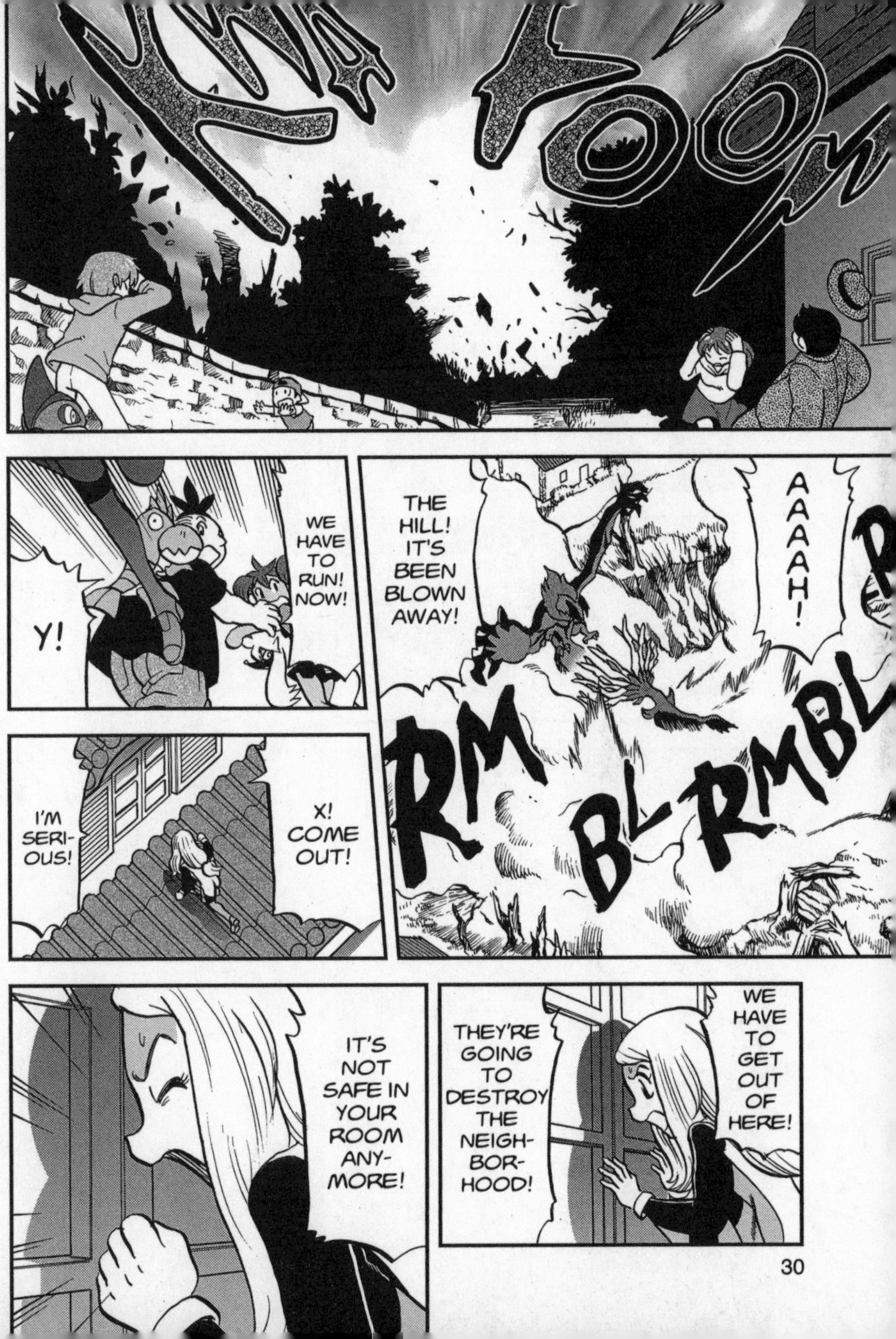

AAAAAH!
THE HILL! IT'S BEEN BLOWN AWAY!
RMBL
RM BLRMBL
WE HAVE TO RUN! NOW!
Y!
X! COME OUT!
I'M SERI-OUS!
WE HAVE TO GET OUT OF HERE!
THEY'RE GOING TO DESTROY THE NEIGH-BOR-HOOD!
IT'S NOT SAFE IN YOUR ROOM ANY-MORE!

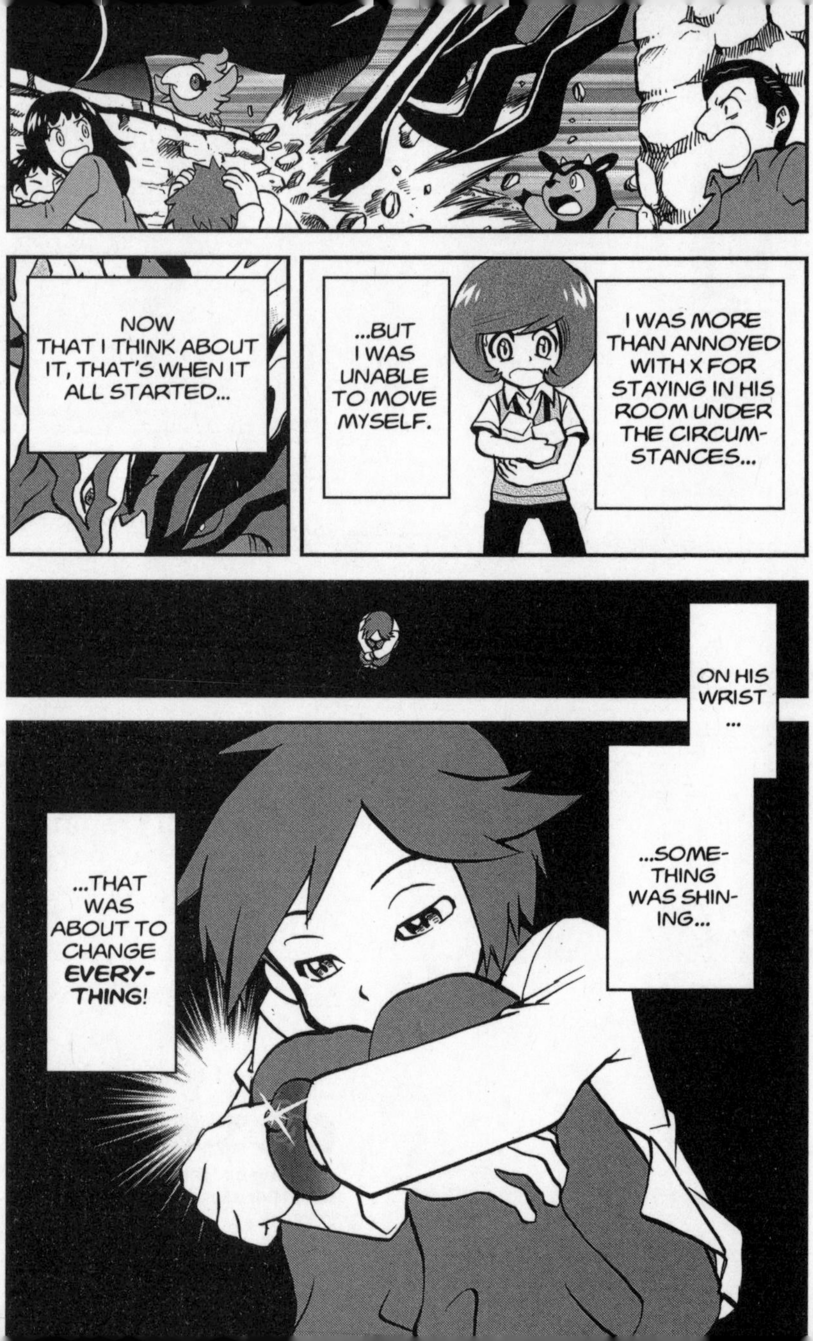
I WAS MORE THAN ANNOYED WITH X FOR STAYING IN HIS ROOM UNDER THE CIRCUM-STANCES...
...BUT I WAS UNABLE TO MOVE MYSELF.
NOW THAT I THINK ABOUT IT, THAT'S WHEN IT ALL STARTED...
ON HIS WRIST...
...SOME-THING WAS SHIN-ING...
...THAT WAS ABOUT TO CHANGE **EVERY-THING!**

## Current Location

**Vaniville Town**

**Blooming buds covered in morning dew
exude hope for the future in this small
town.**

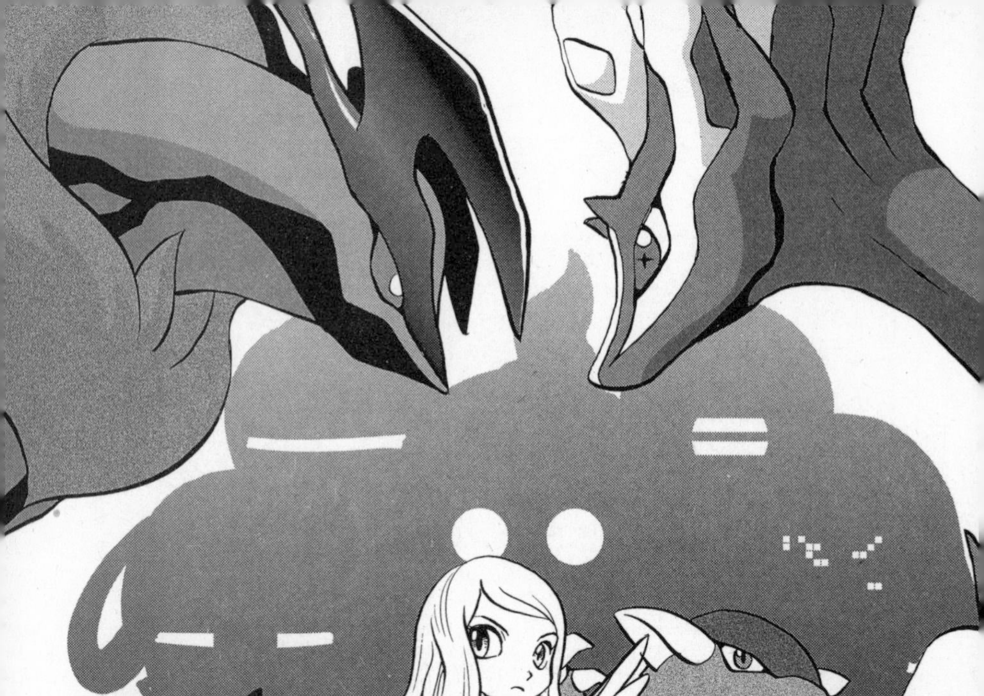

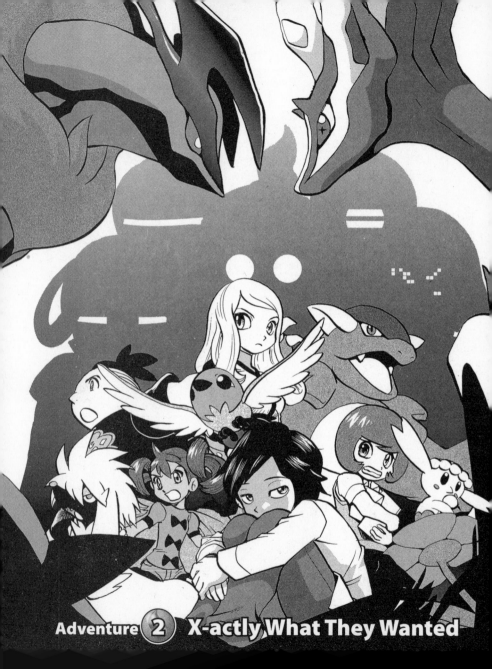

Adventure 2 X-actly What They Wanted

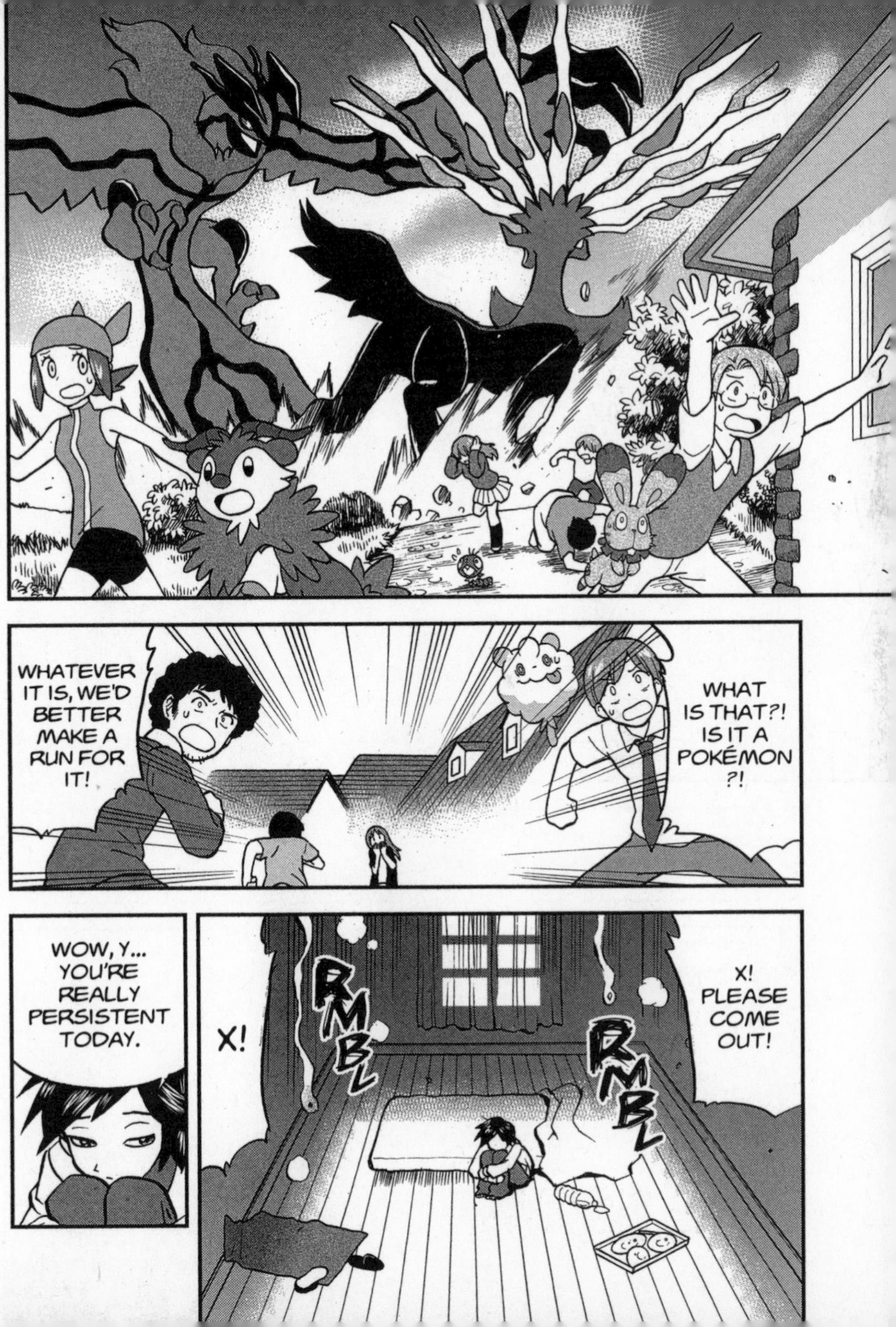
WHAT IS THAT?! IS IT A POKÉMON ?!
WHATEVER IT IS, WE'D BETTER MAKE A RUN FOR IT!
X! PLEASE COME OUT!
RMBL
RMBL
X!
WOW, Y... YOU'RE REALLY PERSISTENT TODAY.

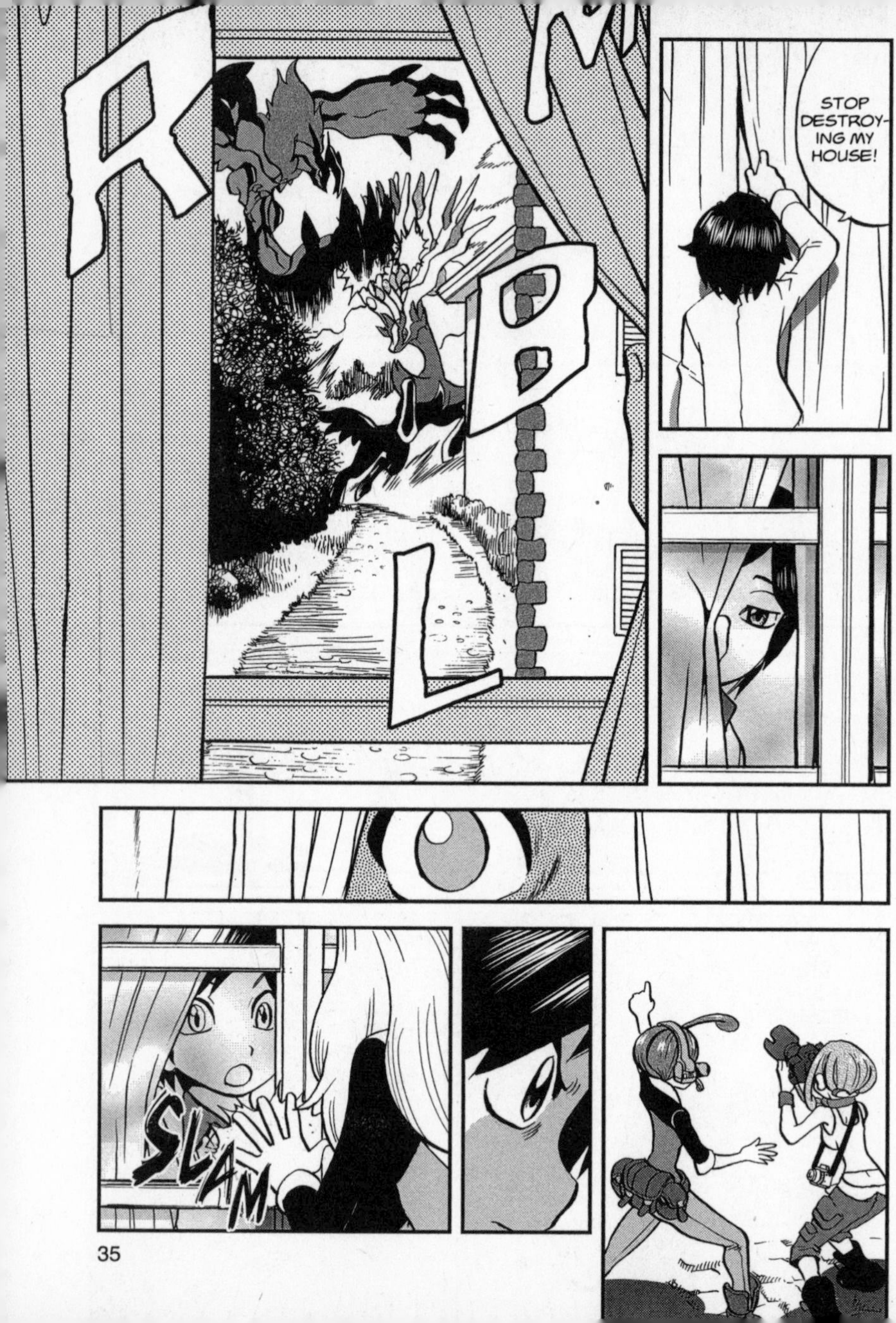
STOP DESTROY-ING MY HOUSE!
RMBL
SLAM

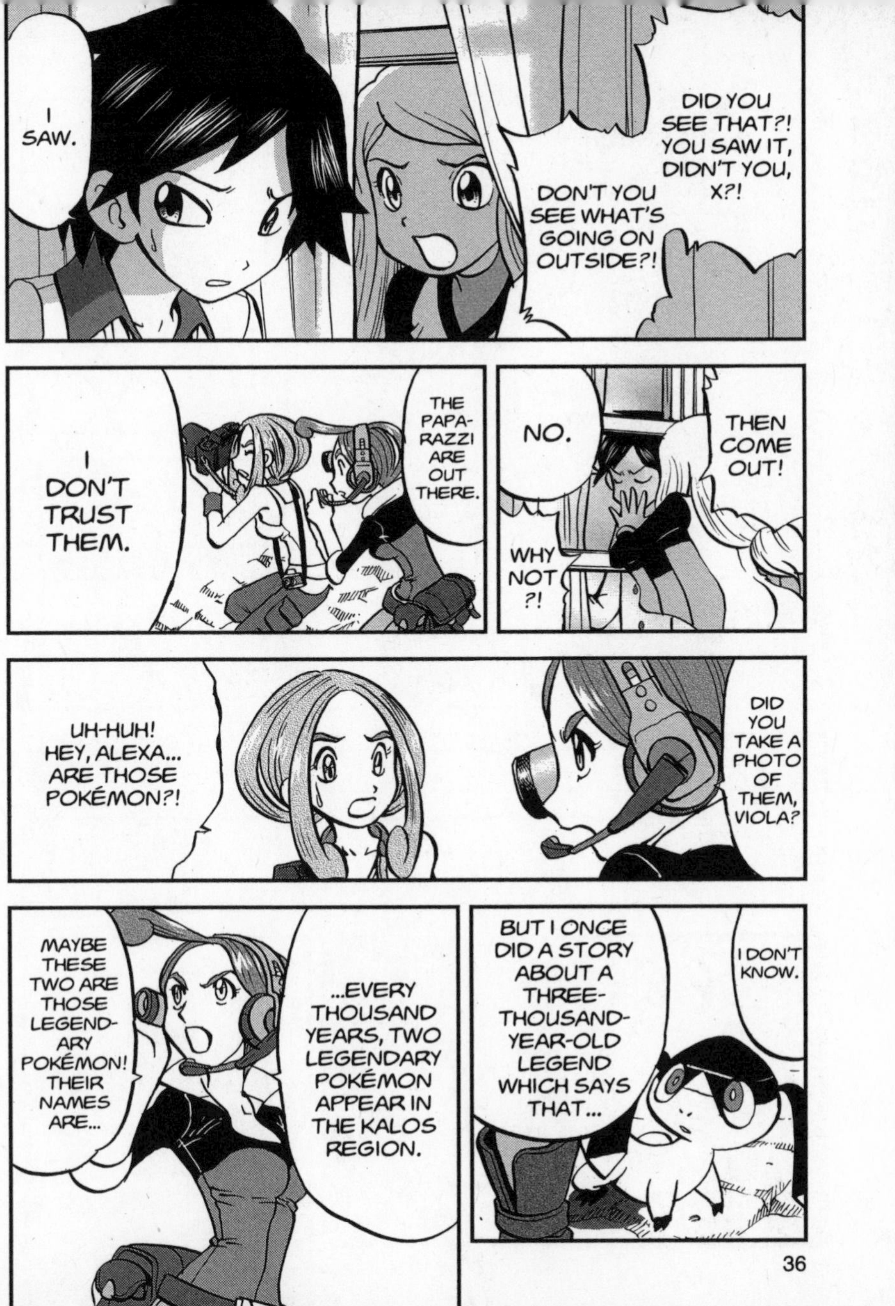
DID YOU SEE THAT?! YOU SAW IT, DIDN'T YOU, X?!
DON'T YOU SEE WHAT'S GOING ON OUTSIDE?!
I SAW.
THEN COME OUT!
NO.
WHY NOT?!
THE PAPARAZZI ARE OUT THERE.
I DON'T TRUST THEM.
DID YOU TAKE A PHOTO OF THEM, VIOLA?
UH-HUH! HEY, ALEXA... ARE THOSE POKÉMON?!
I DON'T KNOW.
BUT I ONCE DID A STORY ABOUT A THREE-THOUSAND-YEAR-OLD LEGEND WHICH SAYS THAT...
...EVERY THOUSAND YEARS, TWO LEGENDARY POKÉMON APPEAR IN THE KALOS REGION.
MAYBE THESE TWO ARE THOSE LEGENDARY POKÉMON! THEIR NAMES ARE...

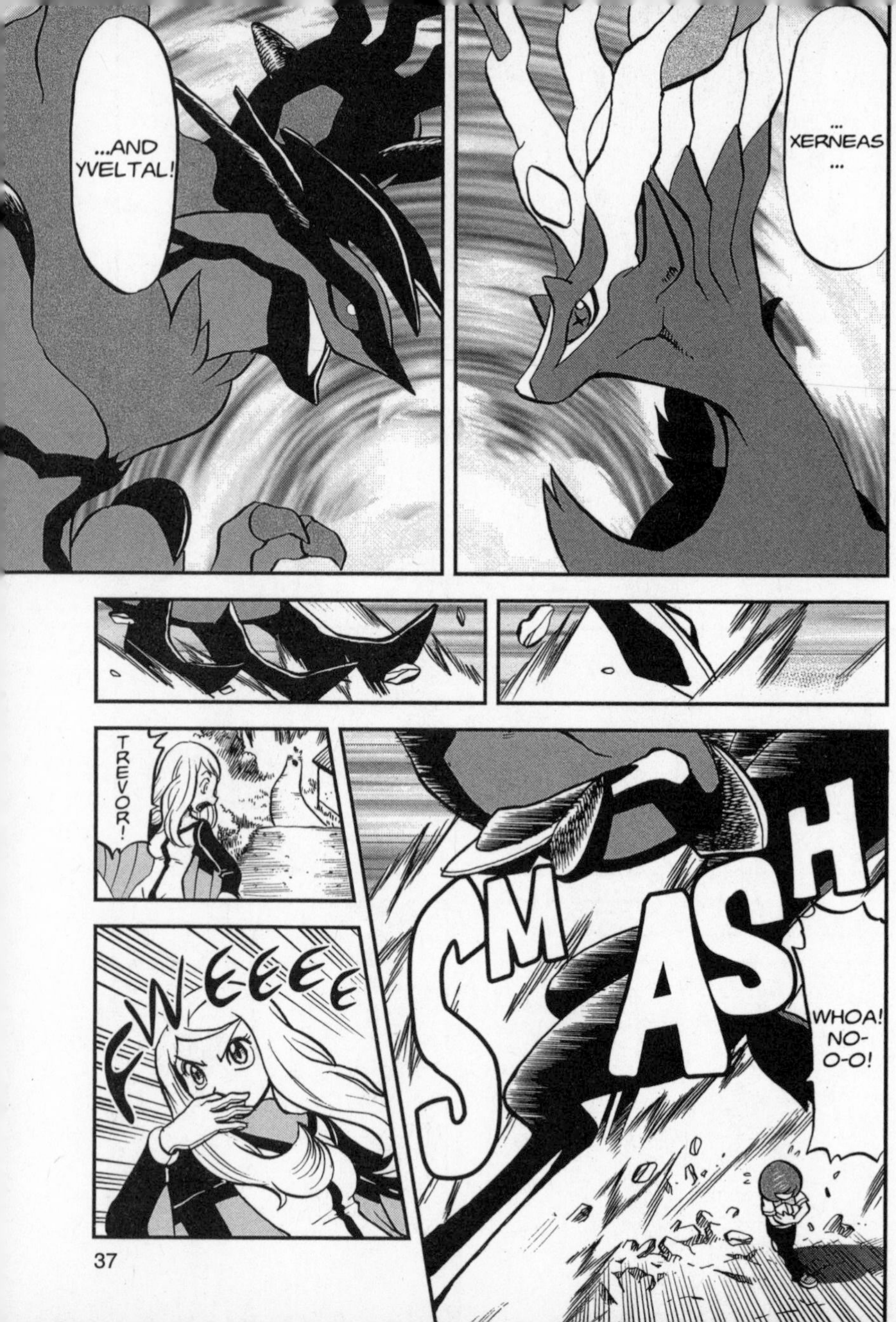
...XERNEAS...
...AND YVELTAL!
SMASH
WHOA! NO-O-O!
TREVOR!
FWEEEEE

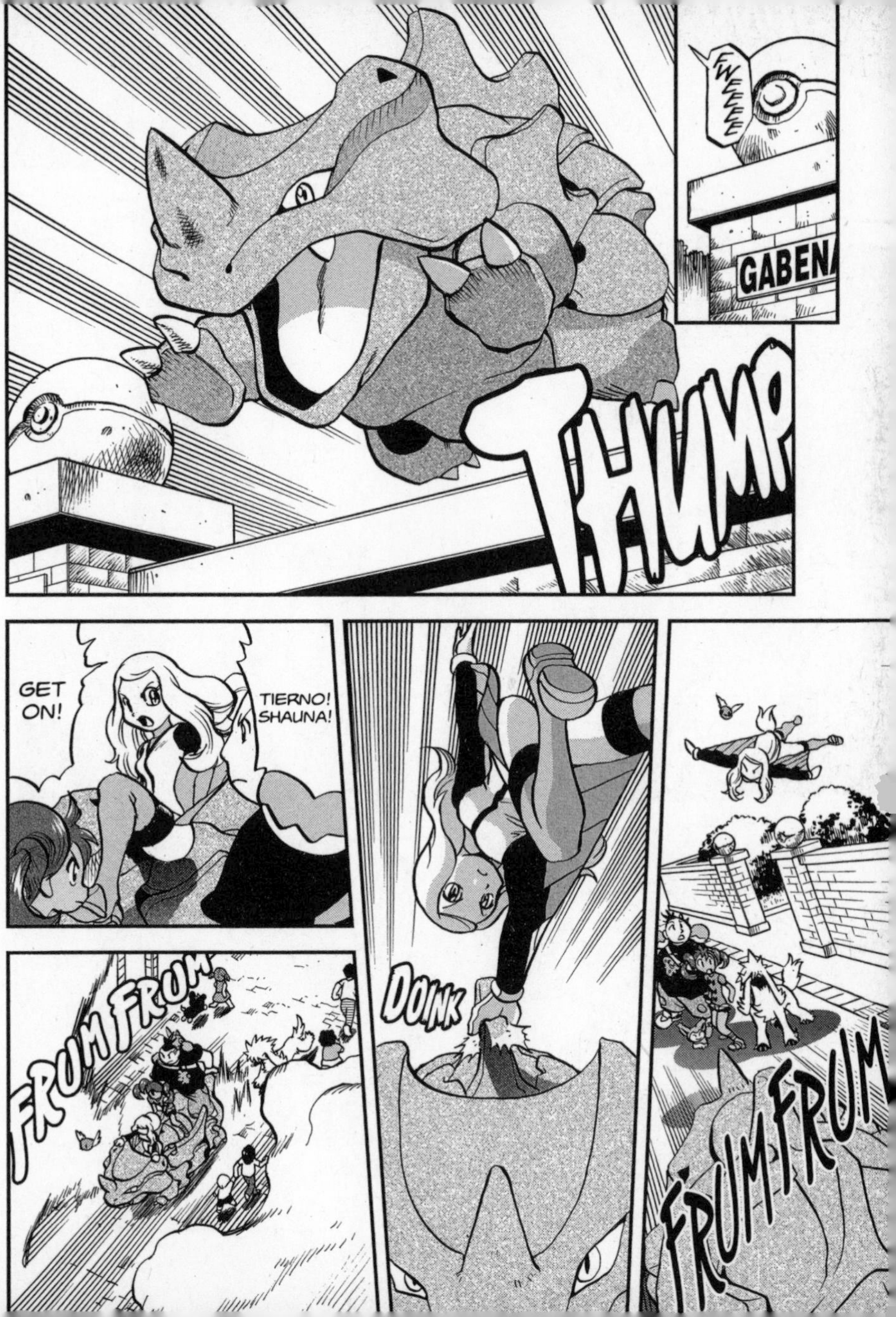
FWEEEE
GABENA
THUMP
FRUM FRUM
DOINK
TIERNO! SHAUNA!
GET ON!
FRUM FRUM

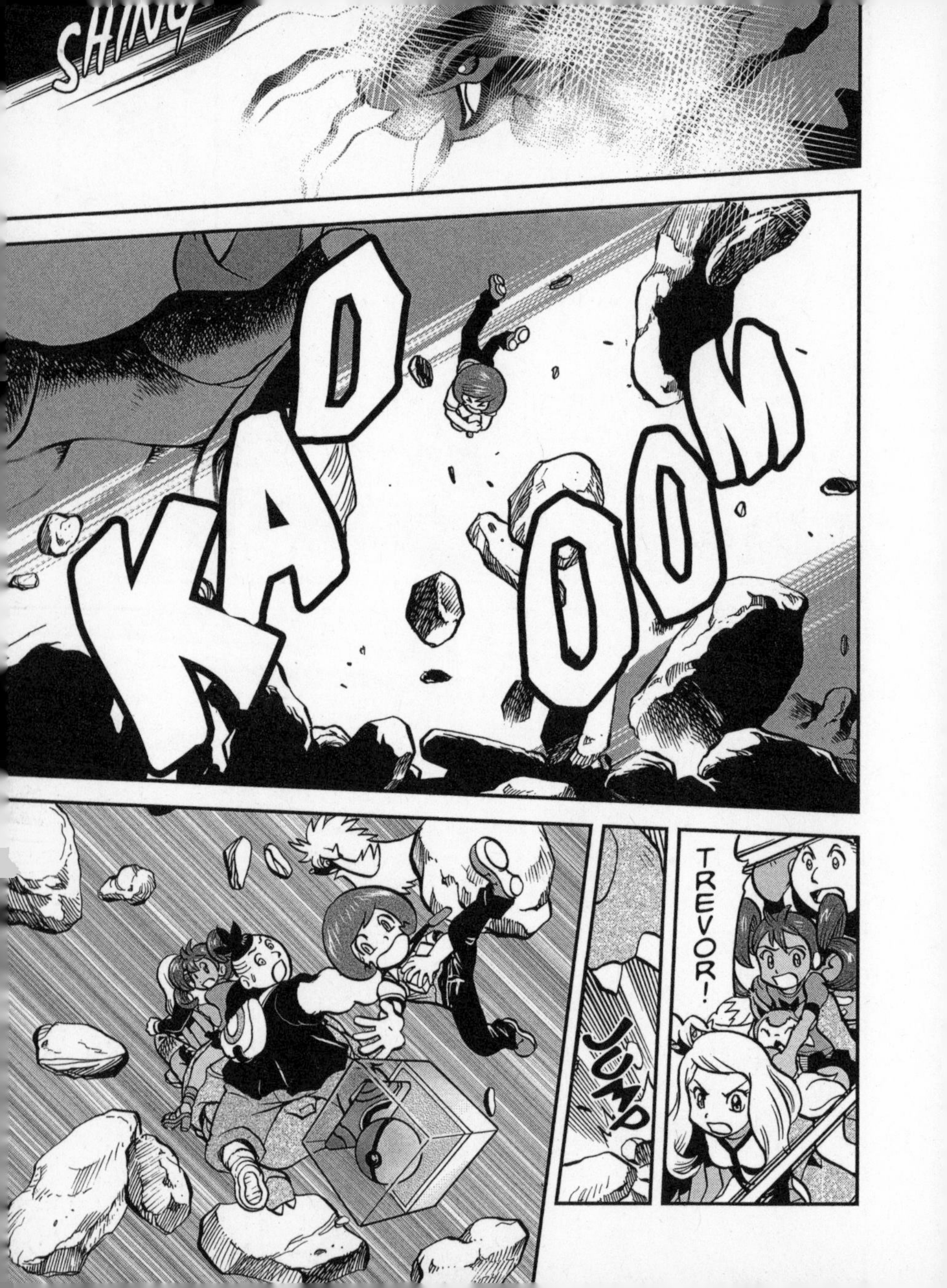
SHING
KA-DOOM
TREVOR!
JUMP

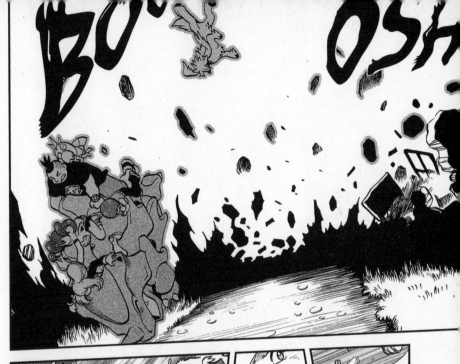

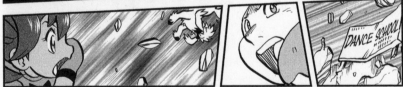

DANCE SCHOOL

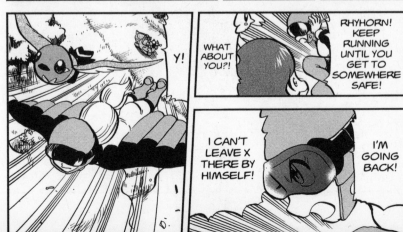

Y!

WHAT ABOUT YOU?!

RHYHORN! KEEP RUNNING UNTIL YOU GET TO SOMEWHERE SAFE!

I CAN'T LEAVE X THERE BY HIMSELF!

I'M GOING BACK!

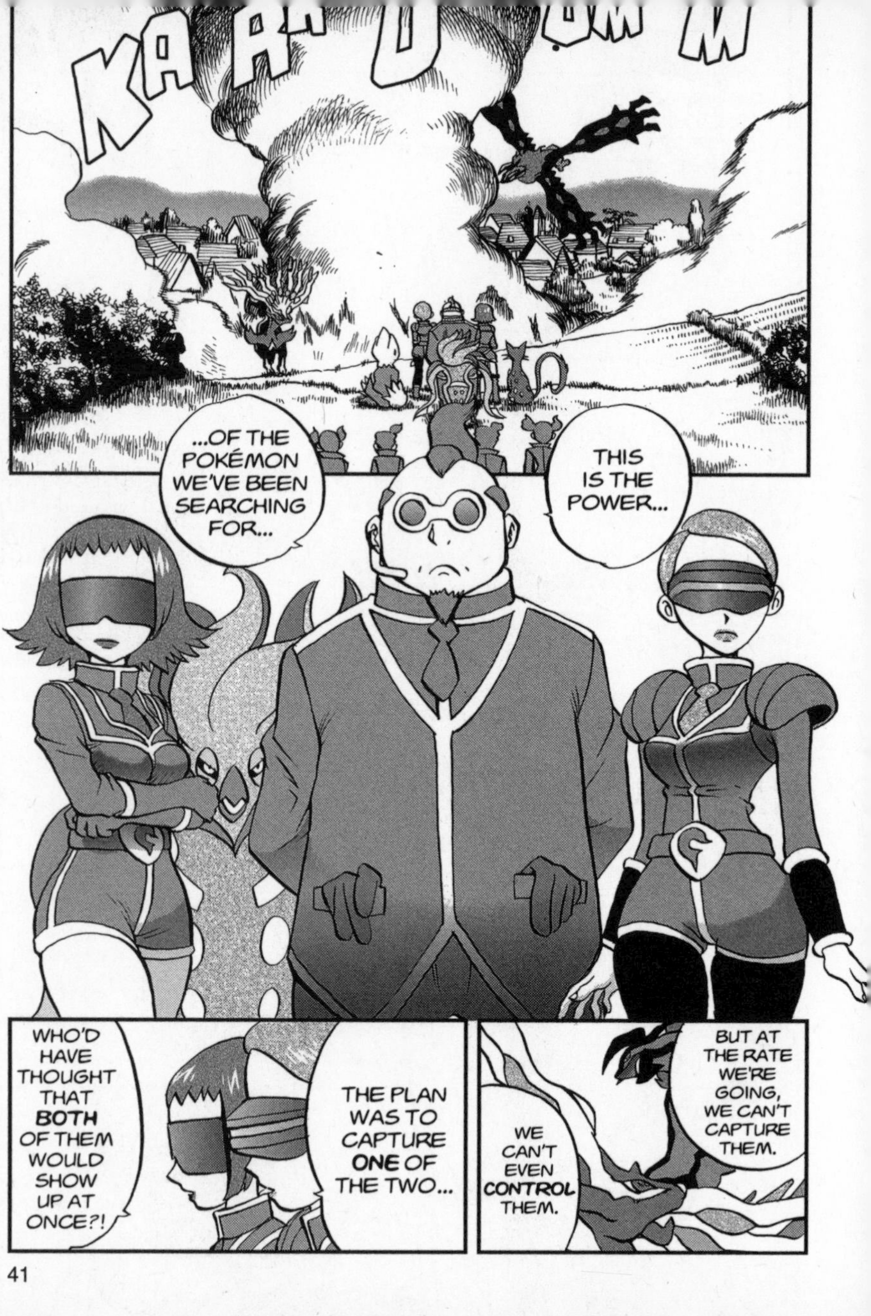
THIS IS THE POWER...
...OF THE POKÉMON WE'VE BEEN SEARCHING FOR...
BUT AT THE RATE WE'RE GOING, WE CAN'T CAPTURE THEM.
WE CAN'T EVEN **CONTROL** THEM.
THE PLAN WAS TO CAPTURE **ONE** OF THE TWO...
WHO'D HAVE THOUGHT THAT **BOTH** OF THEM WOULD SHOW UP AT ONCE?!

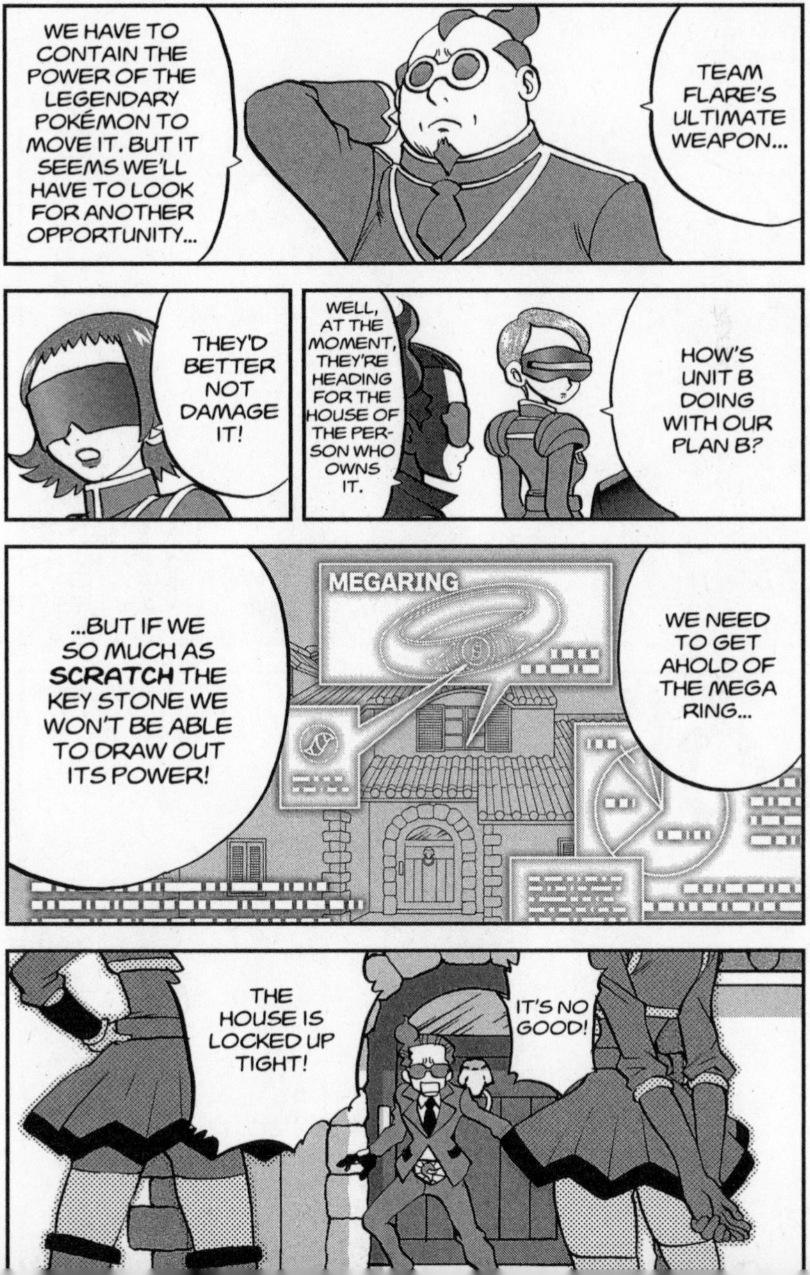
TEAM FLARE'S ULTIMATE WEAPON...
WE HAVE TO CONTAIN THE POWER OF THE LEGENDARY POKÉMON TO MOVE IT. BUT IT SEEMS WE'LL HAVE TO LOOK FOR ANOTHER OPPORTUNITY...
HOW'S UNIT B DOING WITH OUR PLAN B?
WELL, AT THE MOMENT, THEY'RE HEADING FOR THE HOUSE OF THE PERSON WHO OWNS IT.
THEY'D BETTER NOT DAMAGE IT!
WE NEED TO GET AHOLD OF THE MEGA RING...
MEGARING
...BUT IF WE SO MUCH AS **SCRATCH** THE KEY STONE WE WON'T BE ABLE TO DRAW OUT ITS POWER!
IT'S NO GOOD!
THE HOUSE IS LOCKED UP TIGHT!

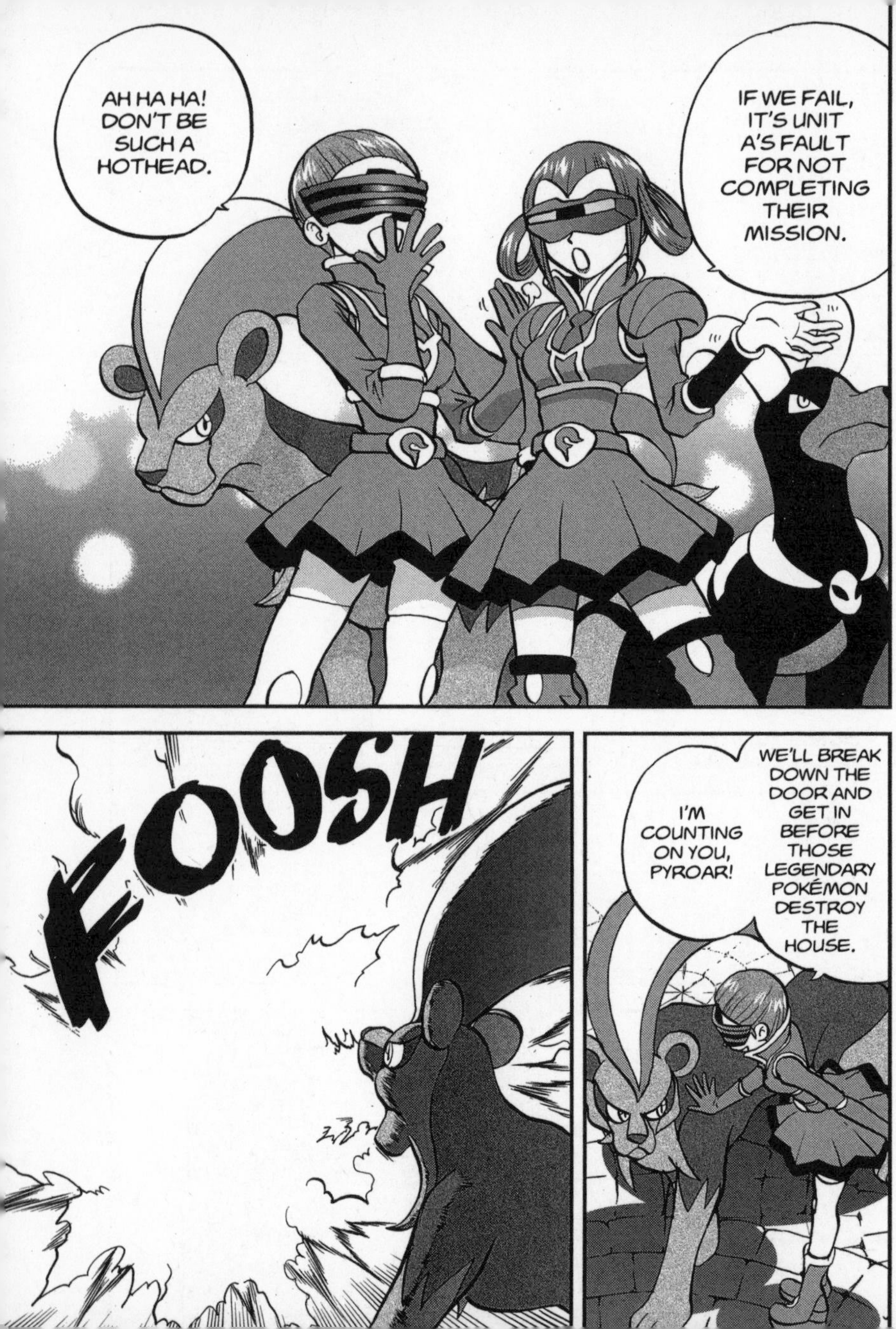
IF WE FAIL, IT'S UNIT A'S FAULT FOR NOT COMPLETING THEIR MISSION.
AH HA HA! DON'T BE SUCH A HOTHEAD.
WE'LL BREAK DOWN THE DOOR AND GET IN BEFORE THOSE LEGENDARY POKÉMON DESTROY THE HOUSE.
I'M COUNTING ON YOU, PYROAR!
FOOSH

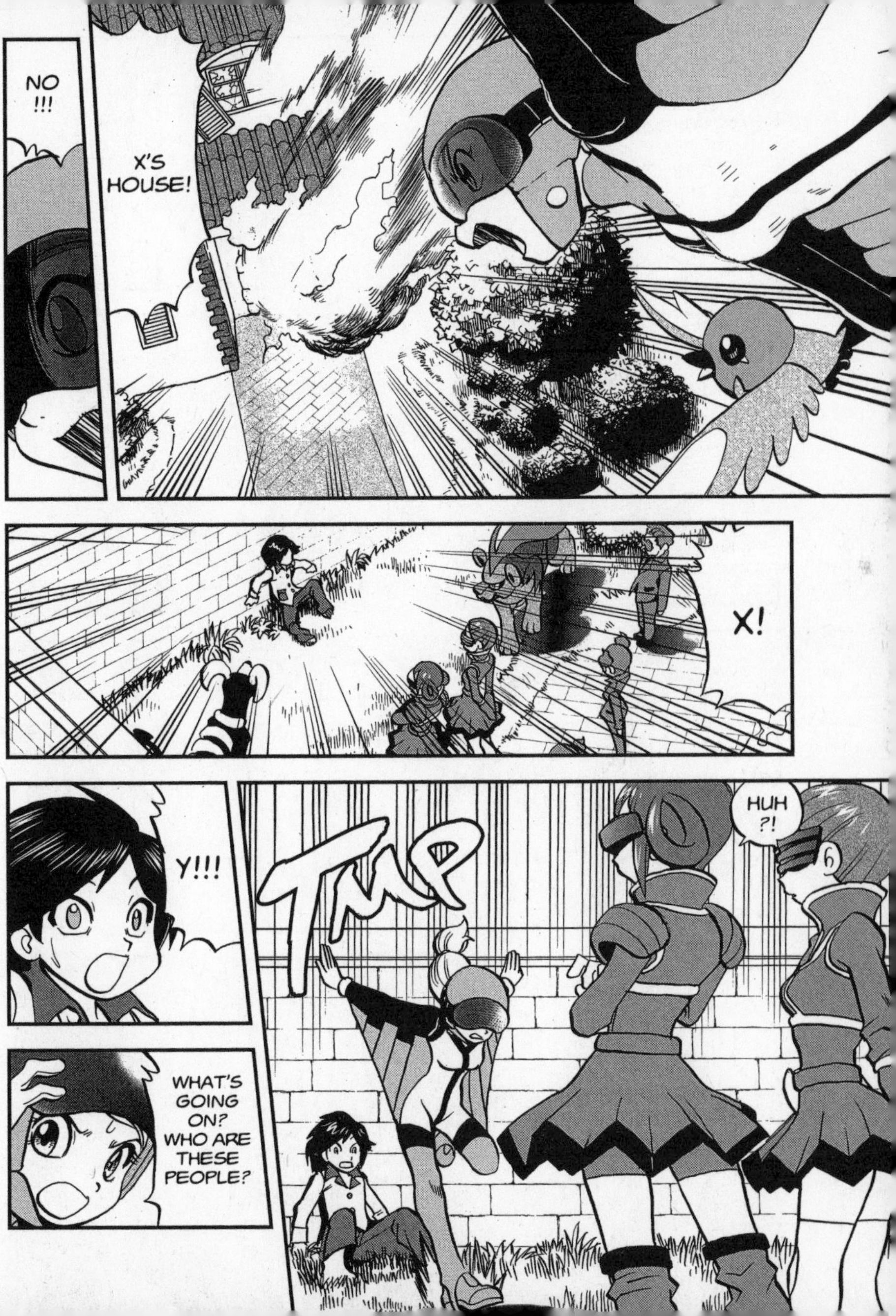
X'S HOUSE!
NO !!!
X!
HUH ?!
TMP
Y!!!
WHAT'S GOING ON? WHO ARE THESE PEOPLE?

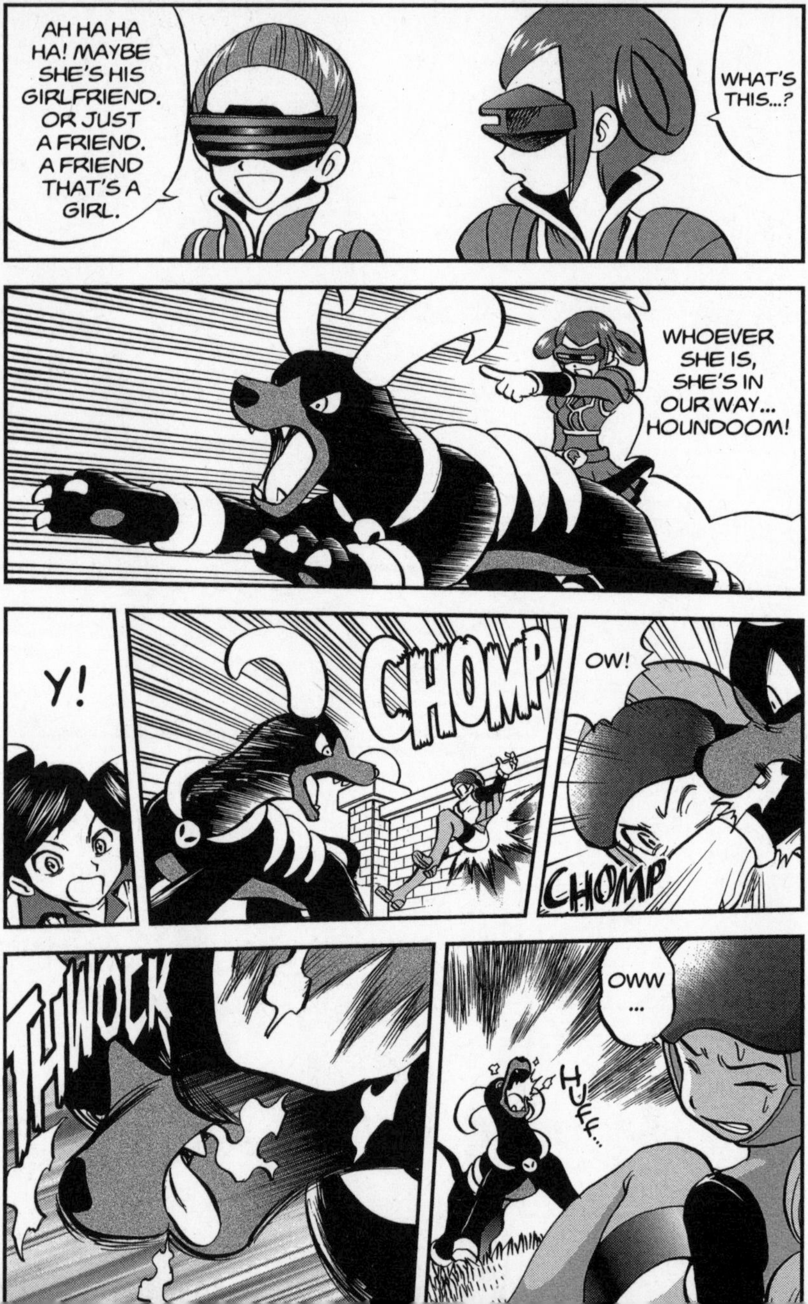
WHAT'S THIS...?
AH HA HA HA! MAYBE SHE'S HIS GIRLFRIEND. OR JUST A FRIEND. A FRIEND THAT'S A GIRL.
WHOEVER SHE IS, SHE'S IN OUR WAY... HOUNDOOM!
OW!
CHOMP
CHOMP
Y!
OWW ...
HUFF...
THWOCK

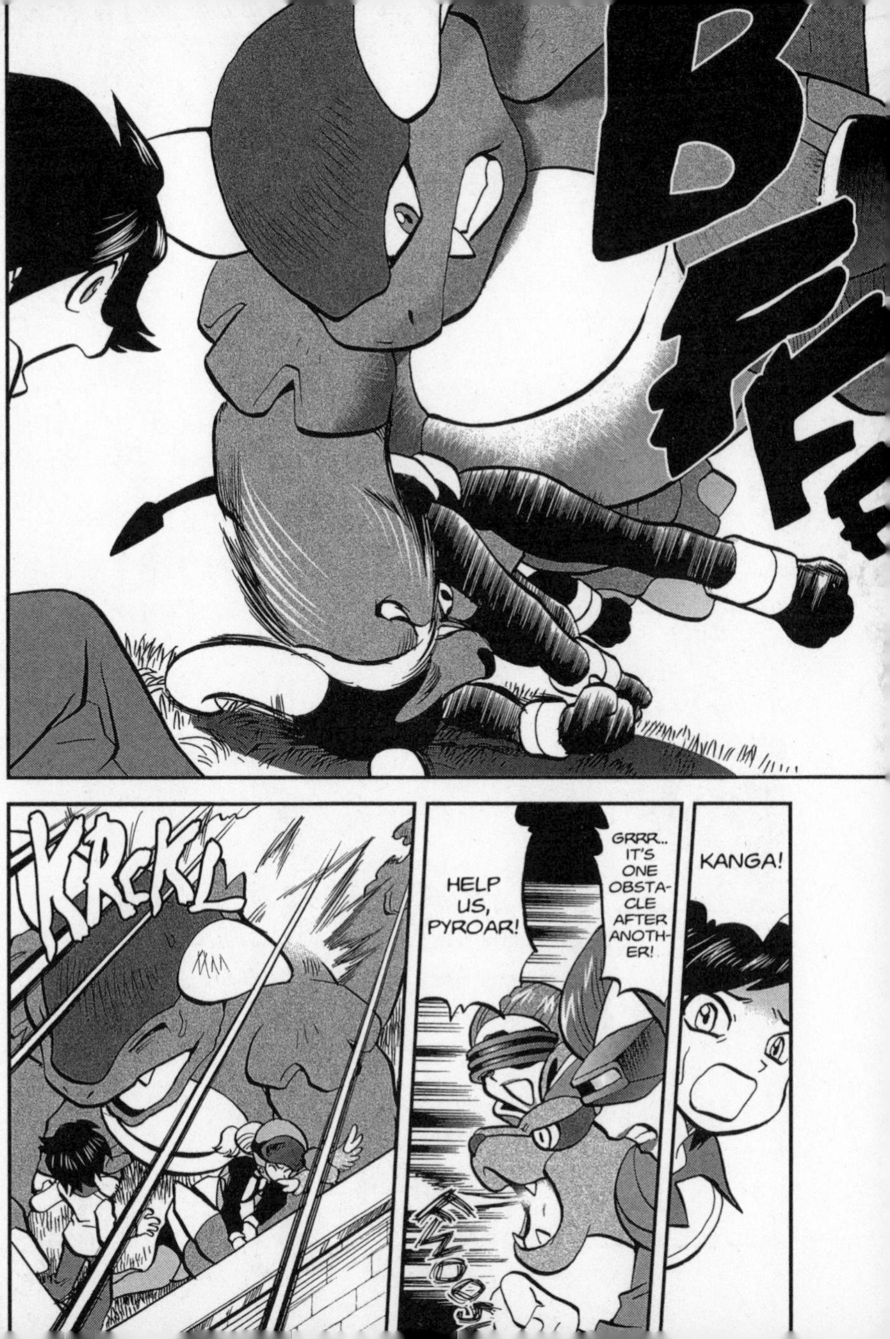
KANGA!
GRRR... IT'S ONE OBSTACLE AFTER ANOTHER!
HELP US, PYROAR!
FWOOSH
KRCKL

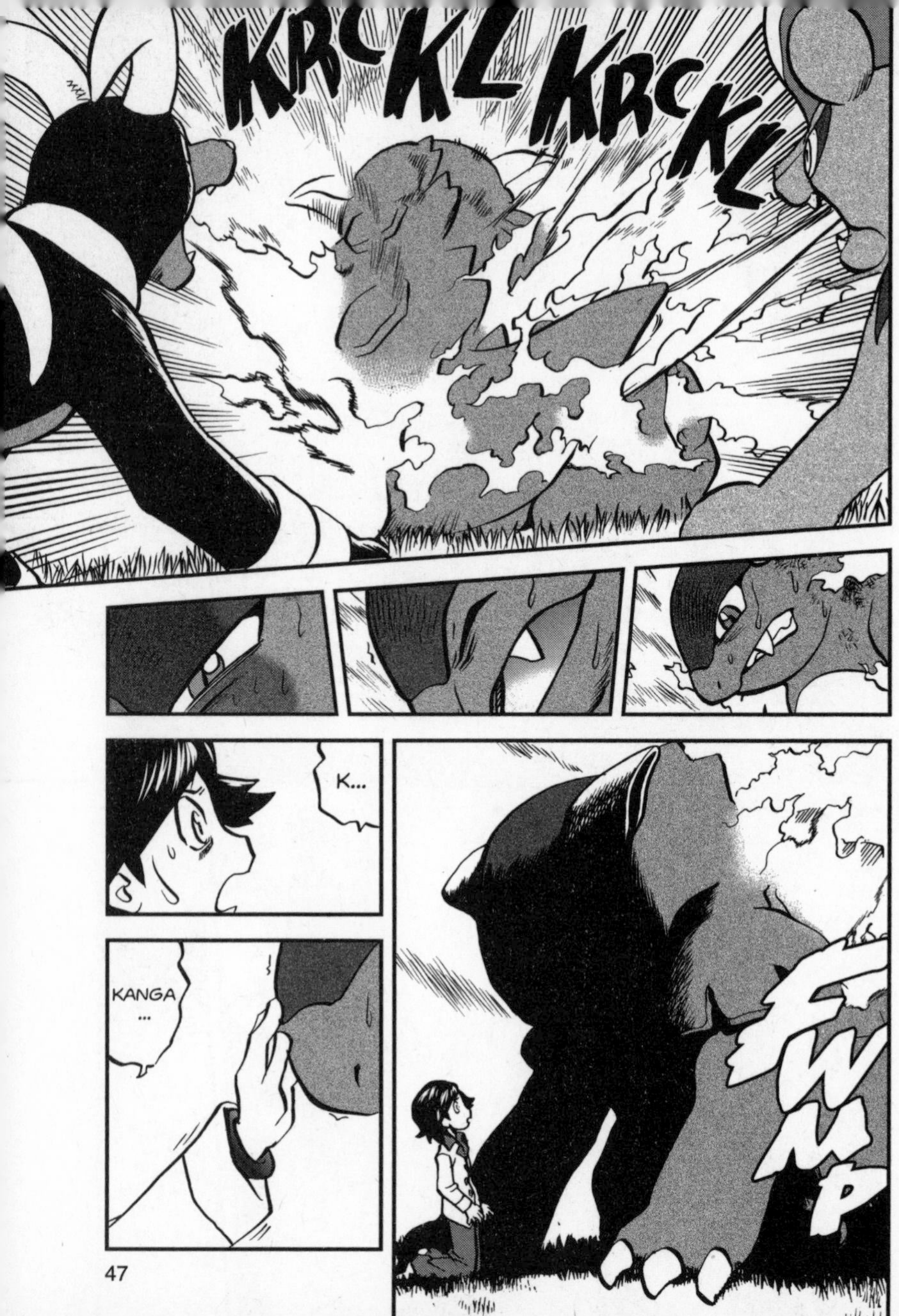
KRCKL KRCKL
FWUMP
K...
KANGA ...

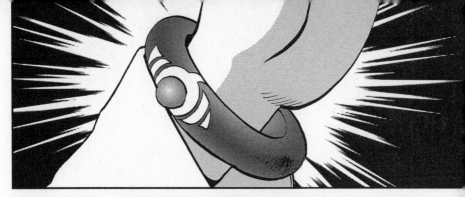

MEGA RING CON-FIRMED!
AH HA HA HA! BRING HIM TO US, PYROAR!
TMPTMP
X...
RSTL
BOOP

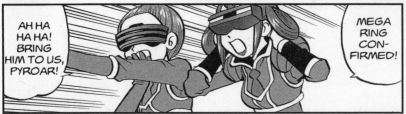

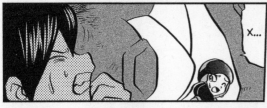

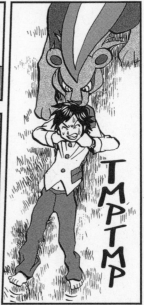

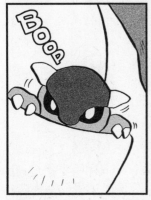

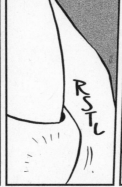

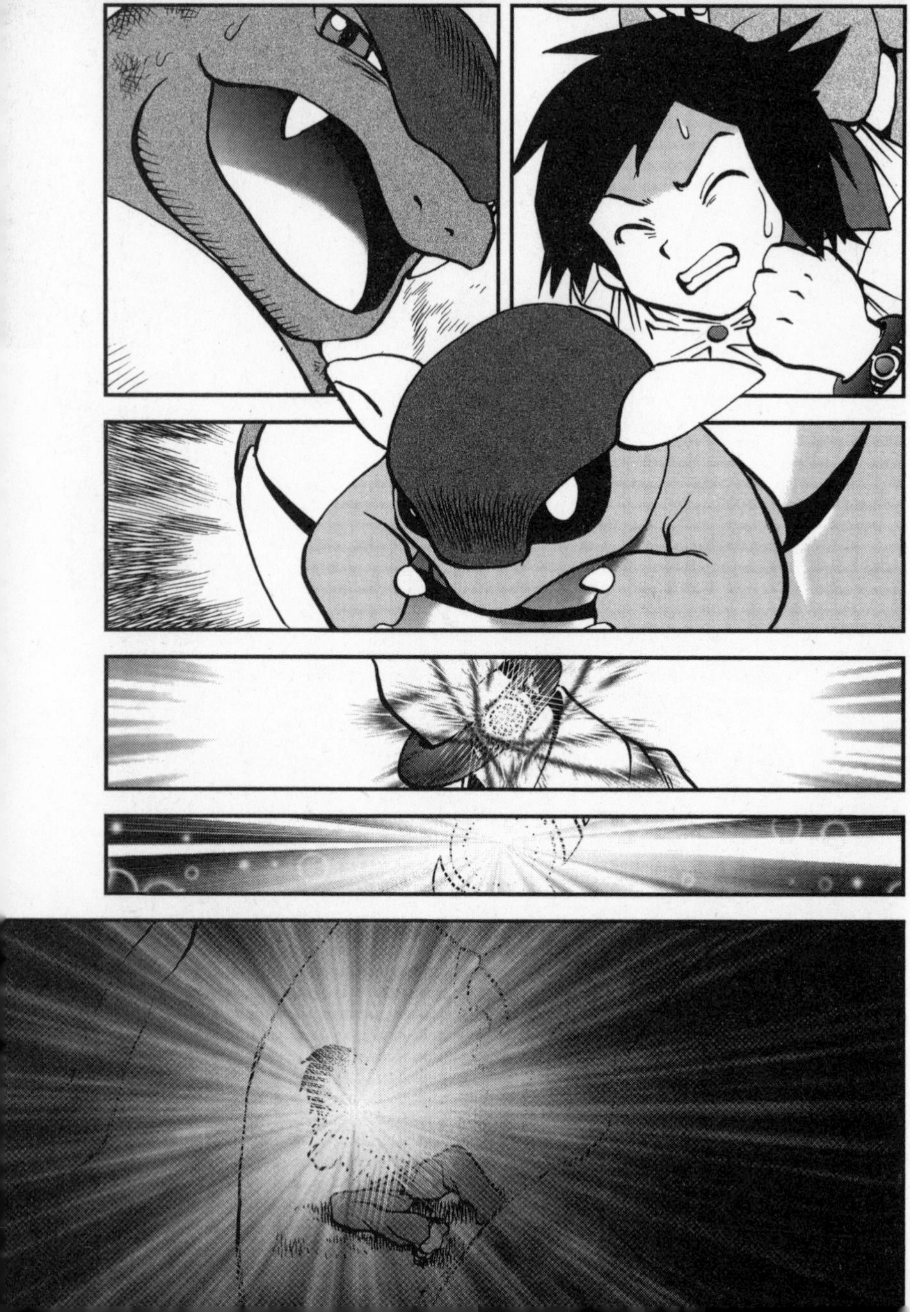

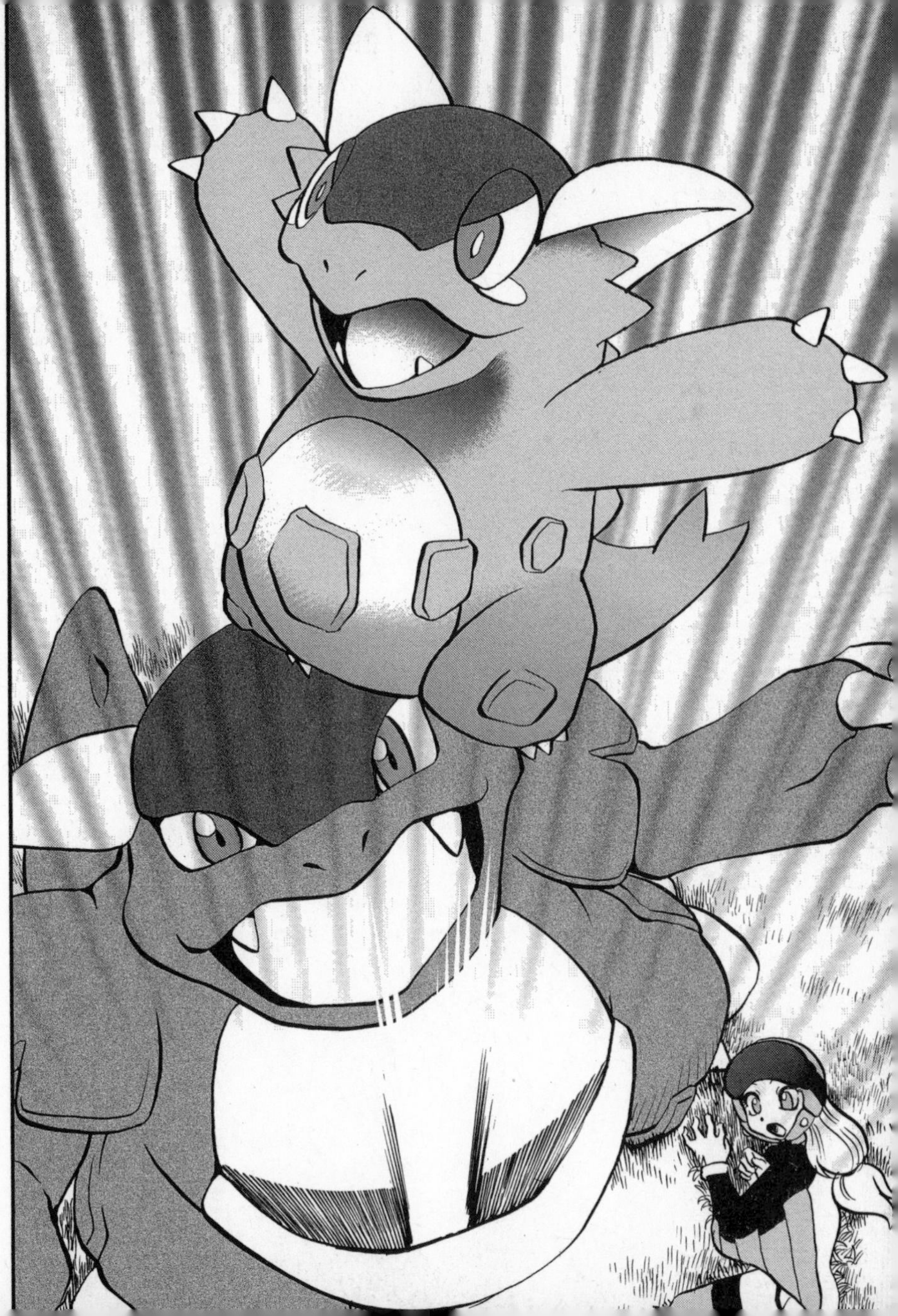

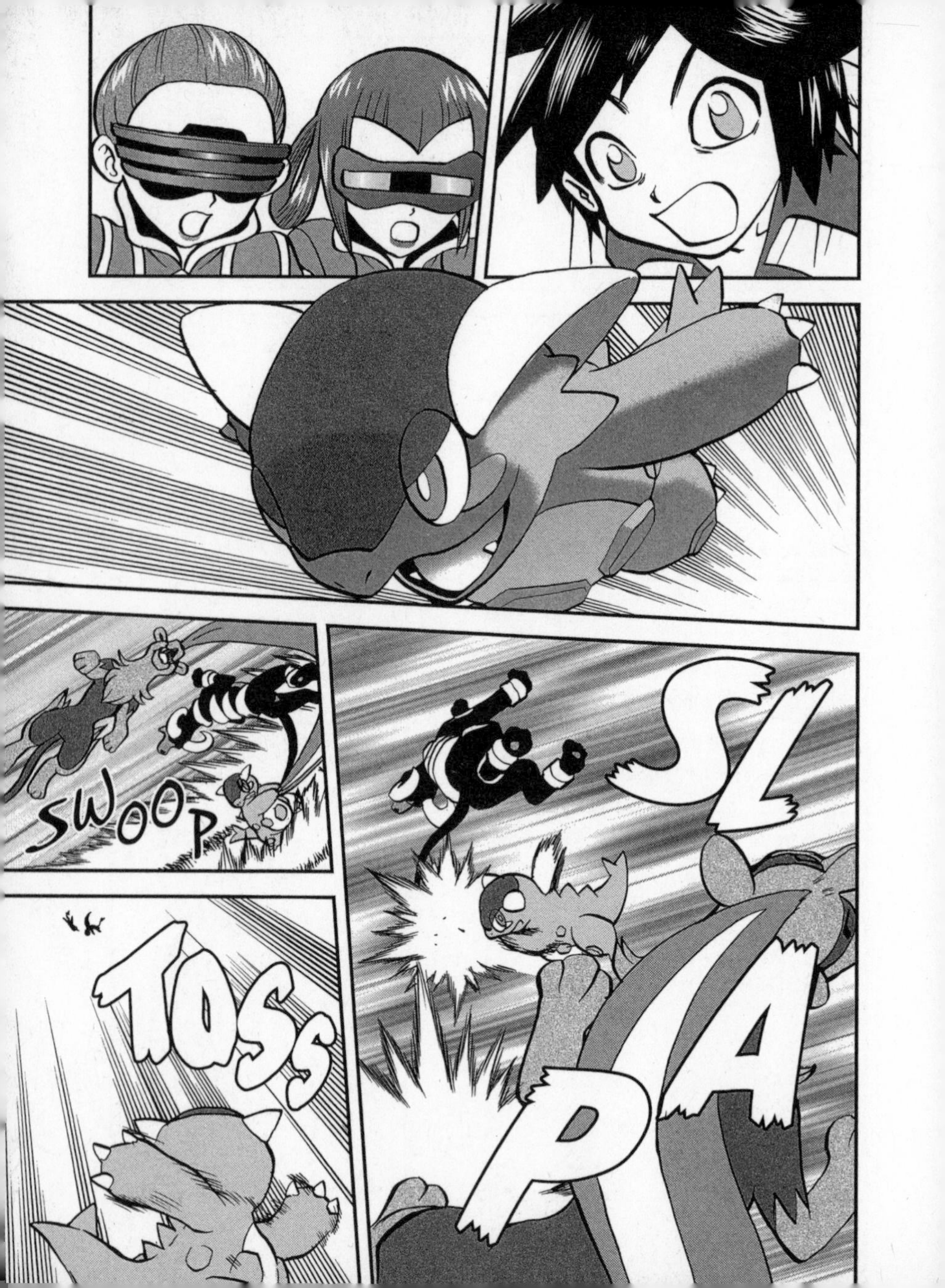
SLAP
SWOOP
TOSS

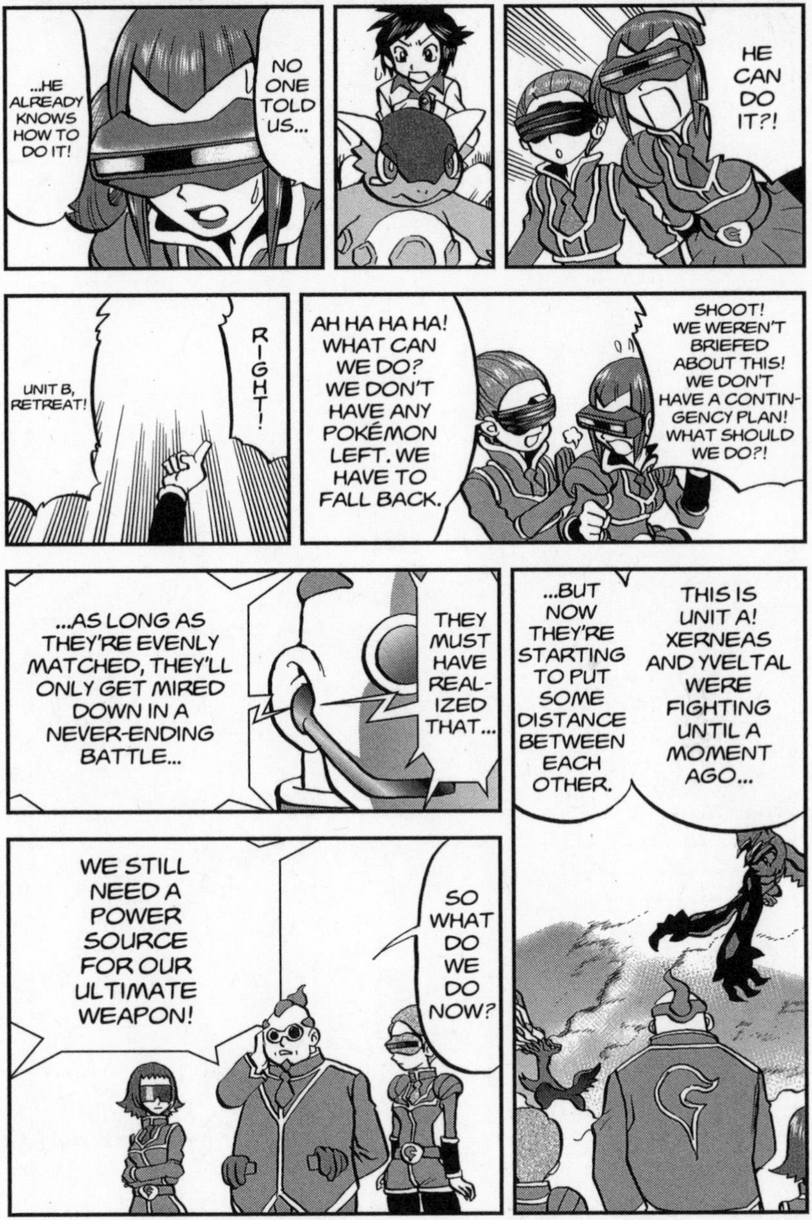
HE CAN DO IT?!
NO ONE TOLD US...
...HE ALREADY KNOWS HOW TO DO IT!
SHOOT! WE WEREN'T BRIEFED ABOUT THIS! WE DON'T HAVE A CONTINGENCY PLAN! WHAT SHOULD WE DO?!
AH HA HA HA! WHAT CAN WE DO? WE DON'T HAVE ANY POKÉMON LEFT. WE HAVE TO FALL BACK.
RIGHT!
UNIT B, RETREAT!
THIS IS UNIT A! XERNEAS AND YVELTAL WERE FIGHTING UNTIL A MOMENT AGO...
...BUT NOW THEY'RE STARTING TO PUT SOME DISTANCE BETWEEN EACH OTHER.
THEY MUST HAVE REALIZED THAT...
...AS LONG AS THEY'RE EVENLY MATCHED, THEY'LL ONLY GET MIRED DOWN IN A NEVER-ENDING BATTLE...
SO WHAT DO WE DO NOW?
WE STILL NEED A POWER SOURCE FOR OUR ULTIMATE WEAPON!

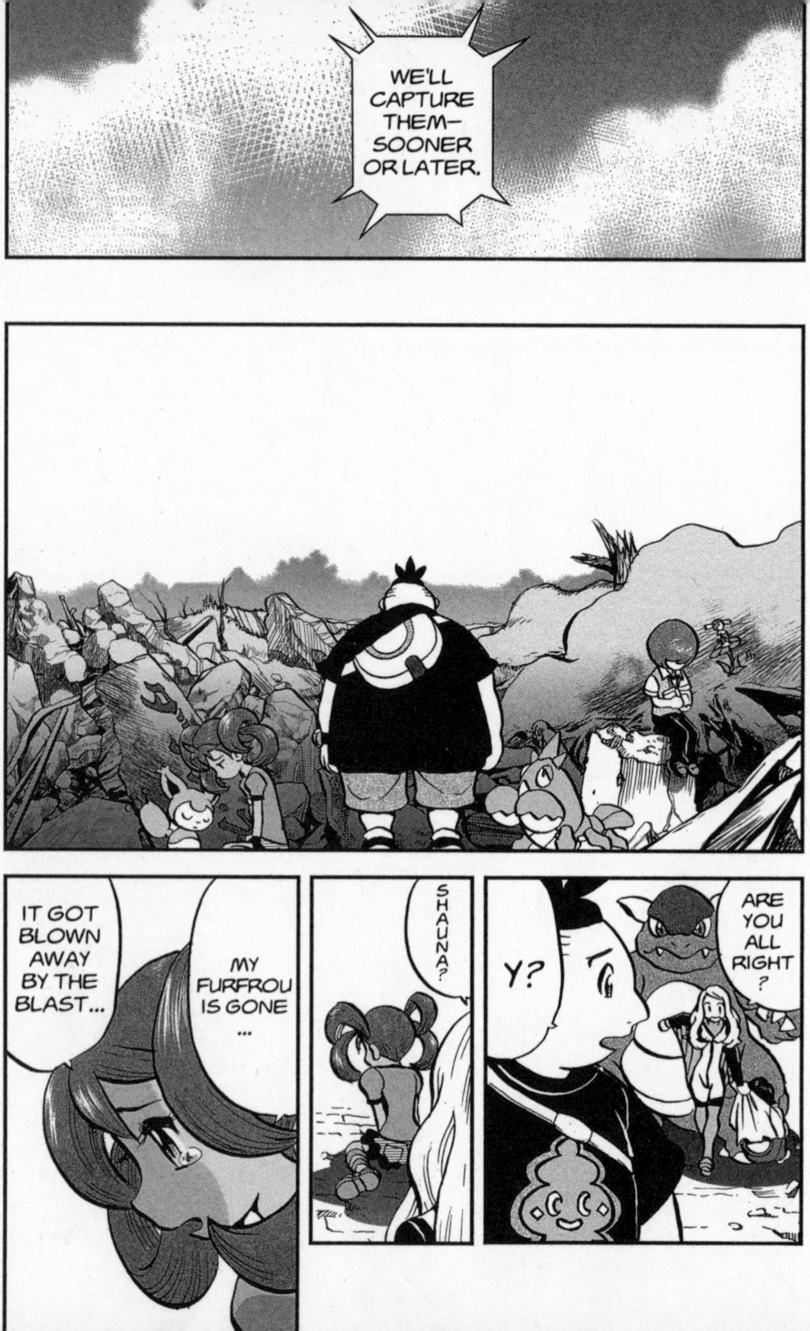
WE'LL CAPTURE THEM— SOONER OR LATER.
ARE YOU ALL RIGHT?
Y?
SHAUNA?
MY FURFROU IS GONE...
IT GOT BLOWN AWAY BY THE BLAST...

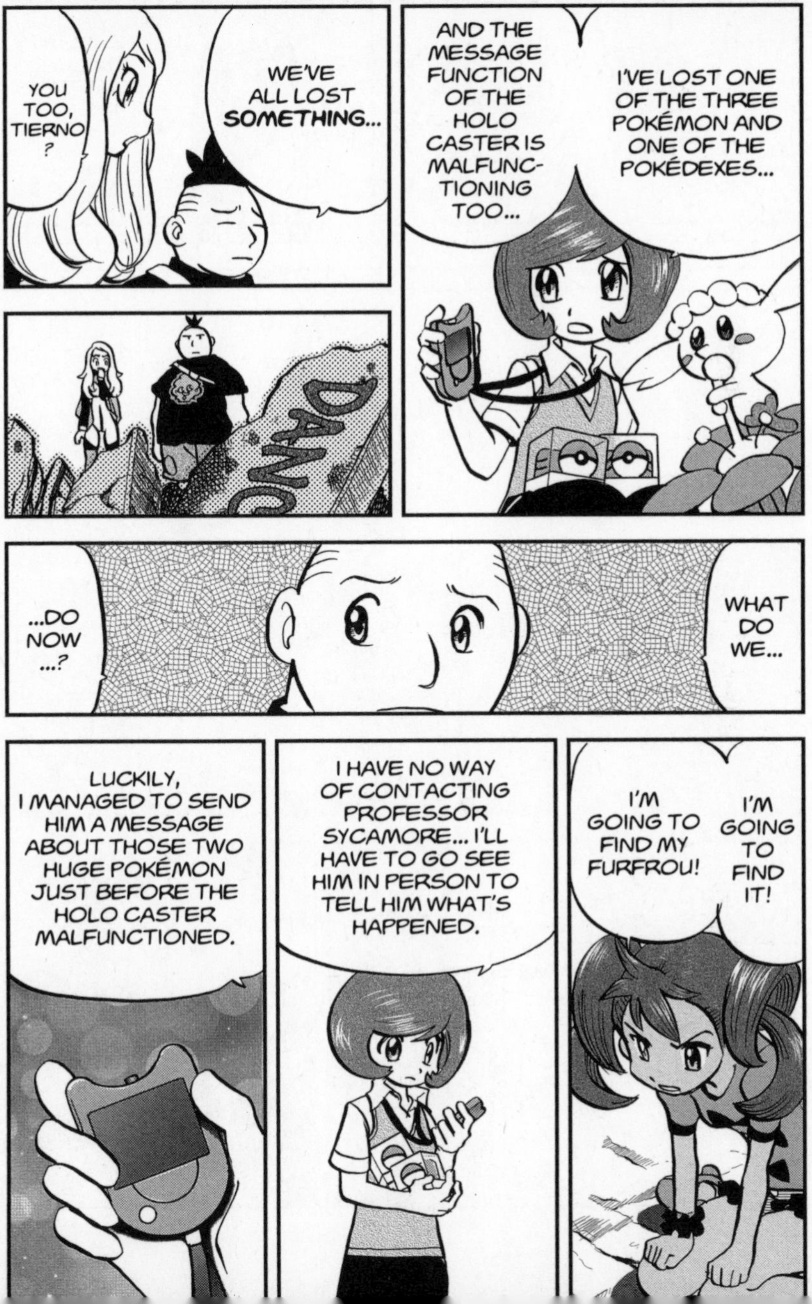
I'VE LOST ONE OF THE THREE POKÉMON AND ONE OF THE POKÉDEXES...
AND THE MESSAGE FUNCTION OF THE HOLO CASTER IS MALFUNCTIONING TOO...
WE'VE ALL LOST **SOMETHING...**
YOU TOO, TIERNO?
WHAT DO WE...
...DO NOW...?
I'M GOING TO FIND IT!
I'M GOING TO FIND MY FURFROU!
I HAVE NO WAY OF CONTACTING PROFESSOR SYCAMORE... I'LL HAVE TO GO SEE HIM IN PERSON TO TELL HIM WHAT'S HAPPENED.
LUCKILY, I MANAGED TO SEND HIM A MESSAGE ABOUT THOSE TWO HUGE POKÉMON JUST BEFORE THE HOLO CASTER MALFUNCTIONED.

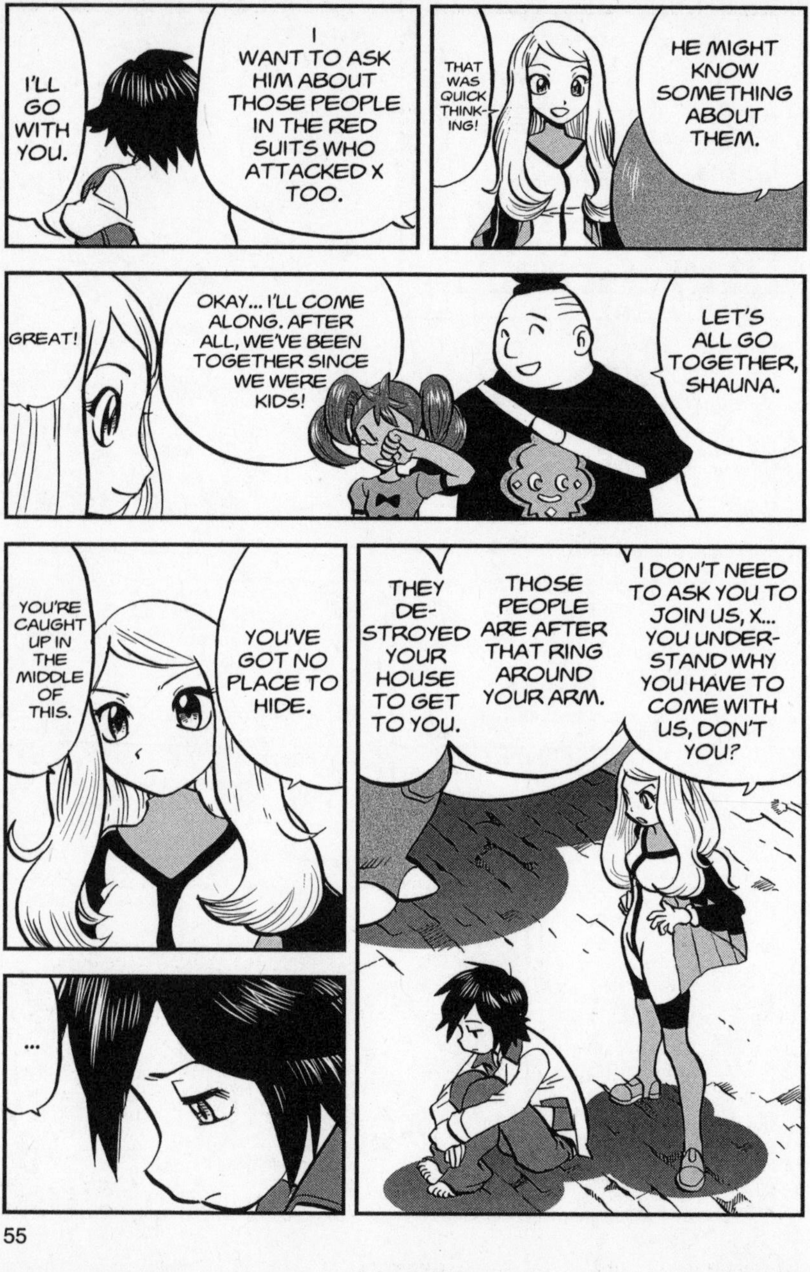
HE MIGHT KNOW SOMETHING ABOUT THEM.
THAT WAS QUICK THINK-ING!
I WANT TO ASK HIM ABOUT THOSE PEOPLE IN THE RED SUITS WHO ATTACKED X TOO.
I'LL GO WITH YOU.
LET'S ALL GO TOGETHER, SHAUNA.
OKAY... I'LL COME ALONG. AFTER ALL, WE'VE BEEN TOGETHER SINCE WE WERE KIDS!
GREAT!
I DON'T NEED TO ASK YOU TO JOIN US, X... YOU UNDER-STAND WHY YOU HAVE TO COME WITH US, DON'T YOU?
THOSE PEOPLE ARE AFTER THAT RING AROUND YOUR ARM.
THEY DE-STROYED YOUR HOUSE TO GET TO YOU.
YOU'VE GOT NO PLACE TO HIDE.
YOU'RE CAUGHT UP IN THE MIDDLE OF THIS.
...

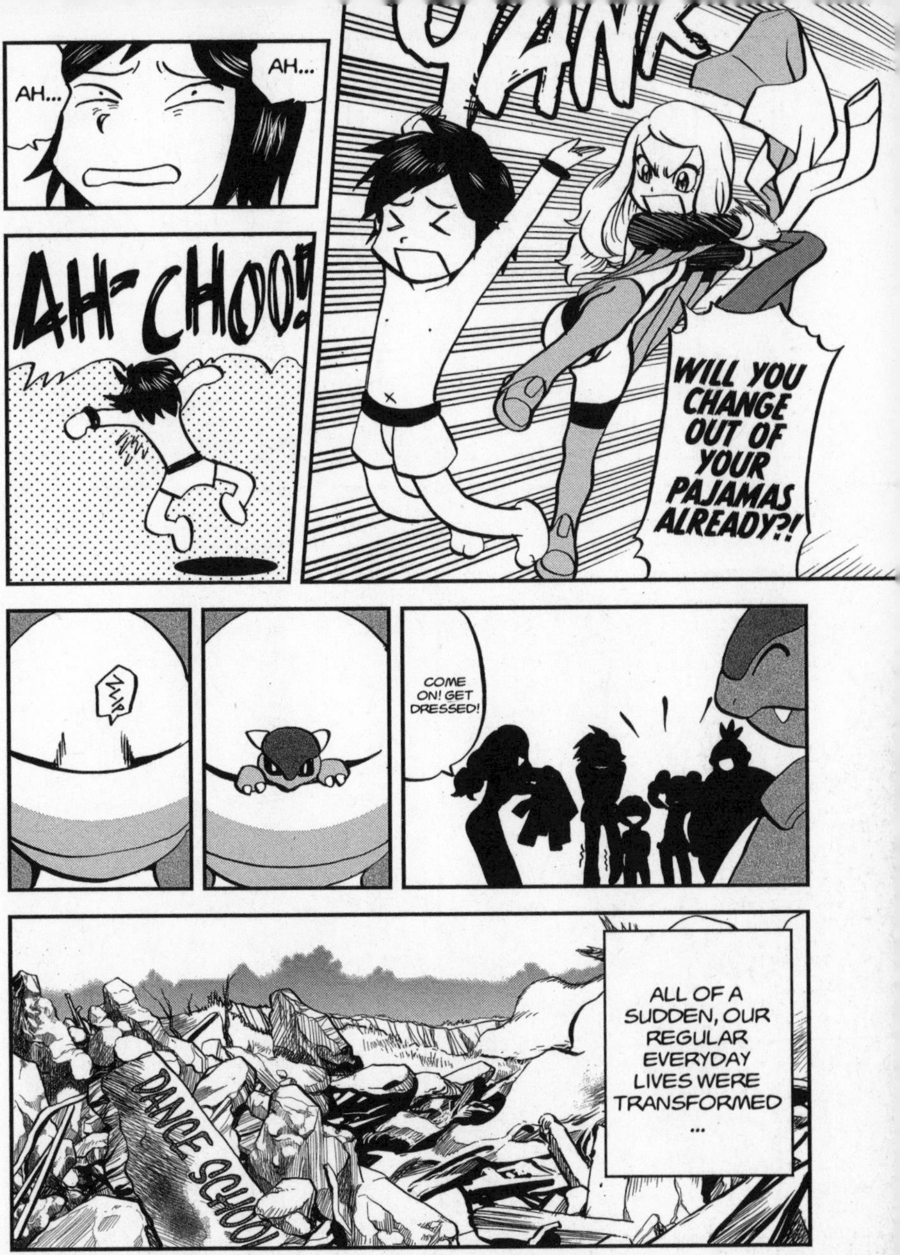
YANK
WILL YOU CHANGE OUT OF YOUR PAJAMAS ALREADY?!
AH...
AH...
AH-CHOO!
COME ON! GET DRESSED!
ZWIP
ALL OF A SUDDEN, OUR REGULAR EVERYDAY LIVES WERE TRANSFORMED ...
DANCE SCHOOL

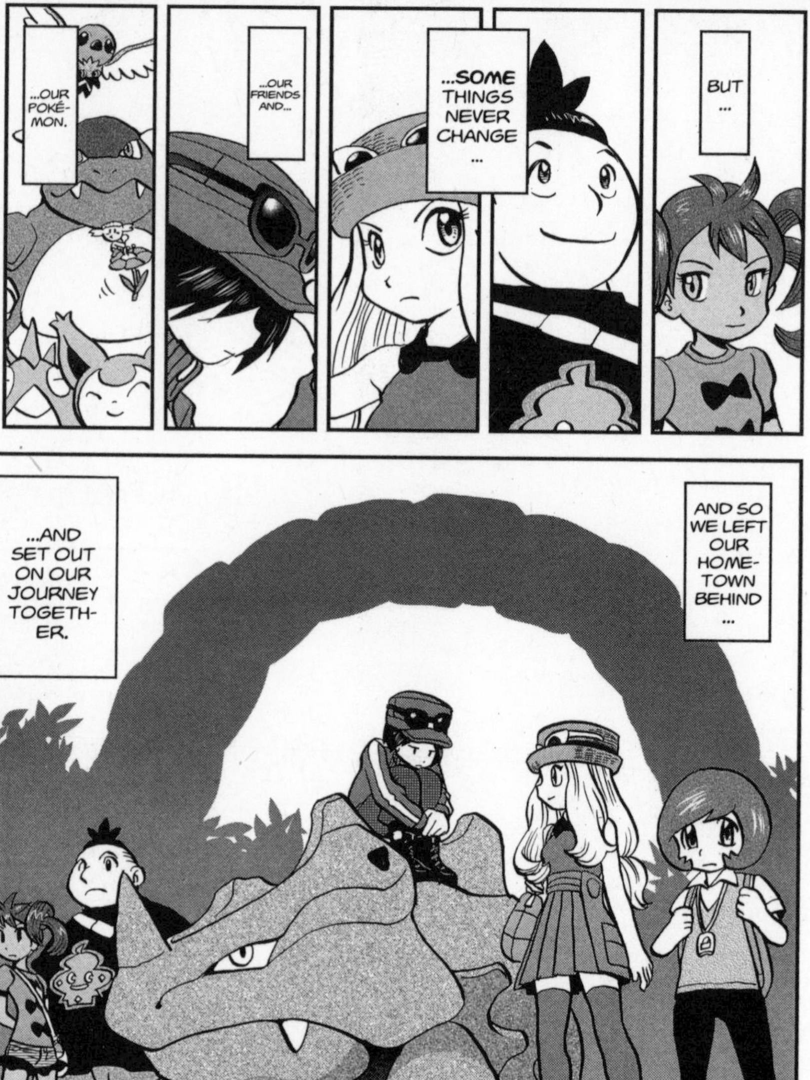
BUT ...
...SOME THINGS NEVER CHANGE ...
...OUR FRIENDS AND...
...OUR POKÉ-MON.
AND SO WE LEFT OUR HOME-TOWN BEHIND ...
...AND SET OUT ON OUR JOURNEY TOGETH-ER.

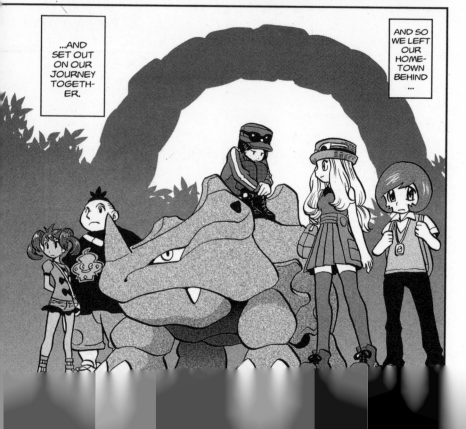

## Current Location

**Vaniville Town**

**Blooming buds covered in morning dew exude hope for the future in this small town.**

# Adventure 3 Inn-teresting Developments

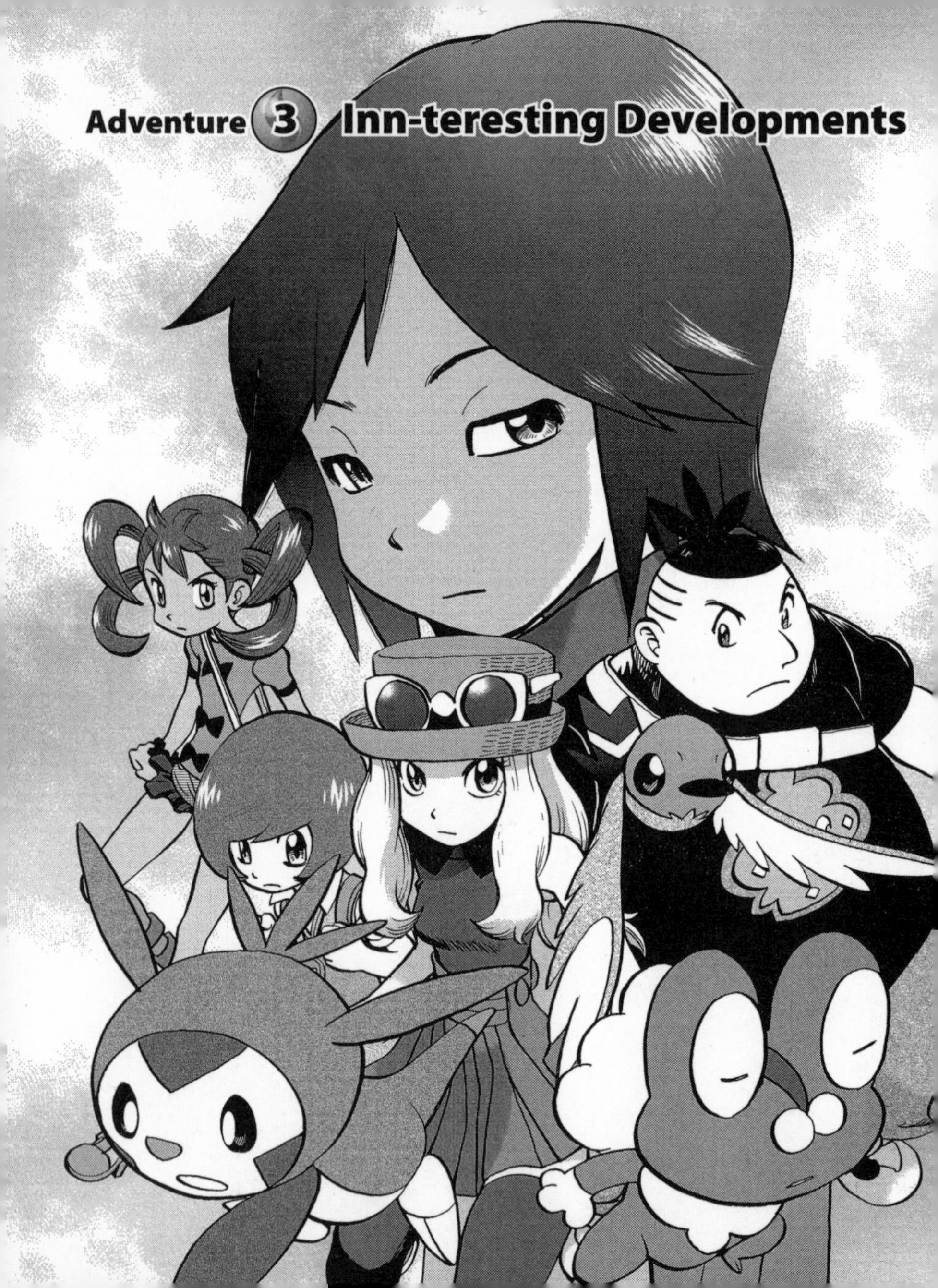

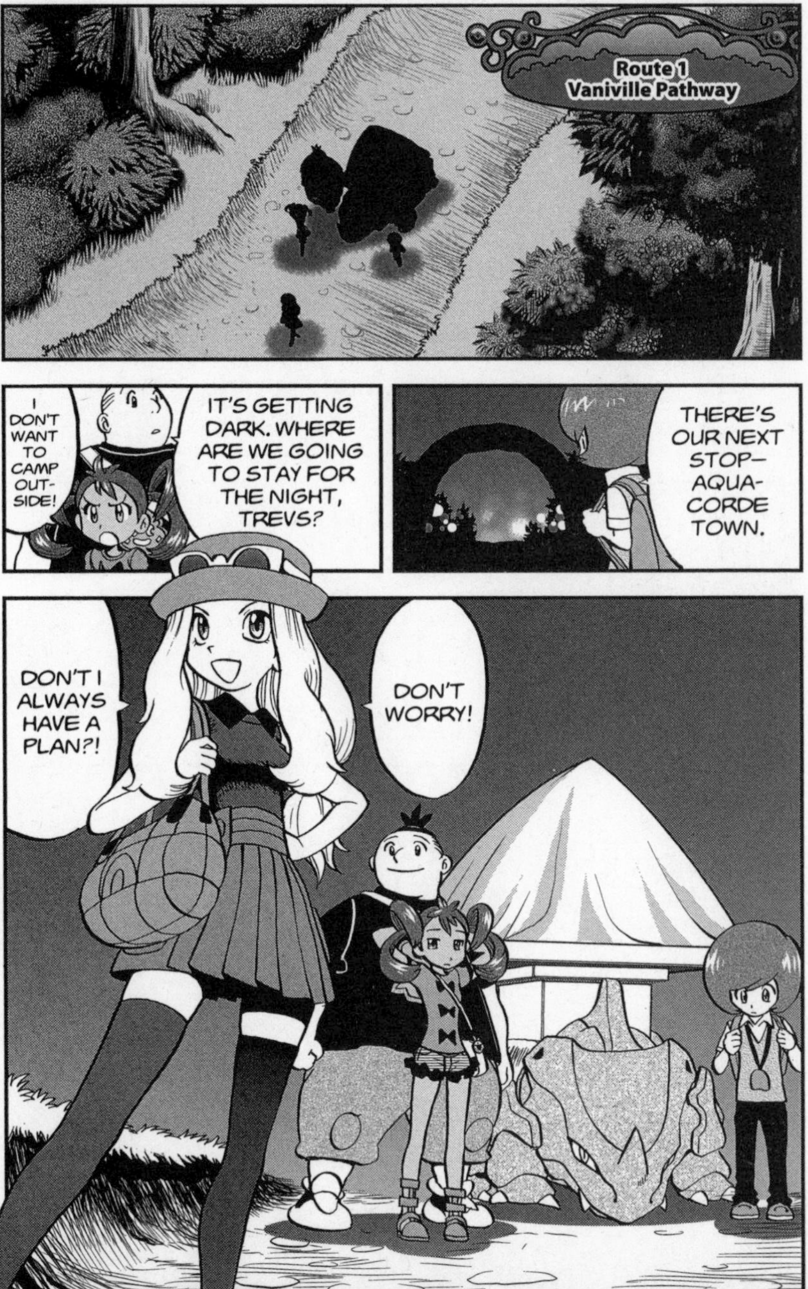
Route 1
Vaniville Pathway
THERE'S OUR NEXT STOP—AQUA-CORDE TOWN.
IT'S GETTING DARK. WHERE ARE WE GOING TO STAY FOR THE NIGHT, TREVS?
I DON'T WANT TO CAMP OUT-SIDE!
DON'T WORRY!
DON'T I ALWAYS HAVE A PLAN?!

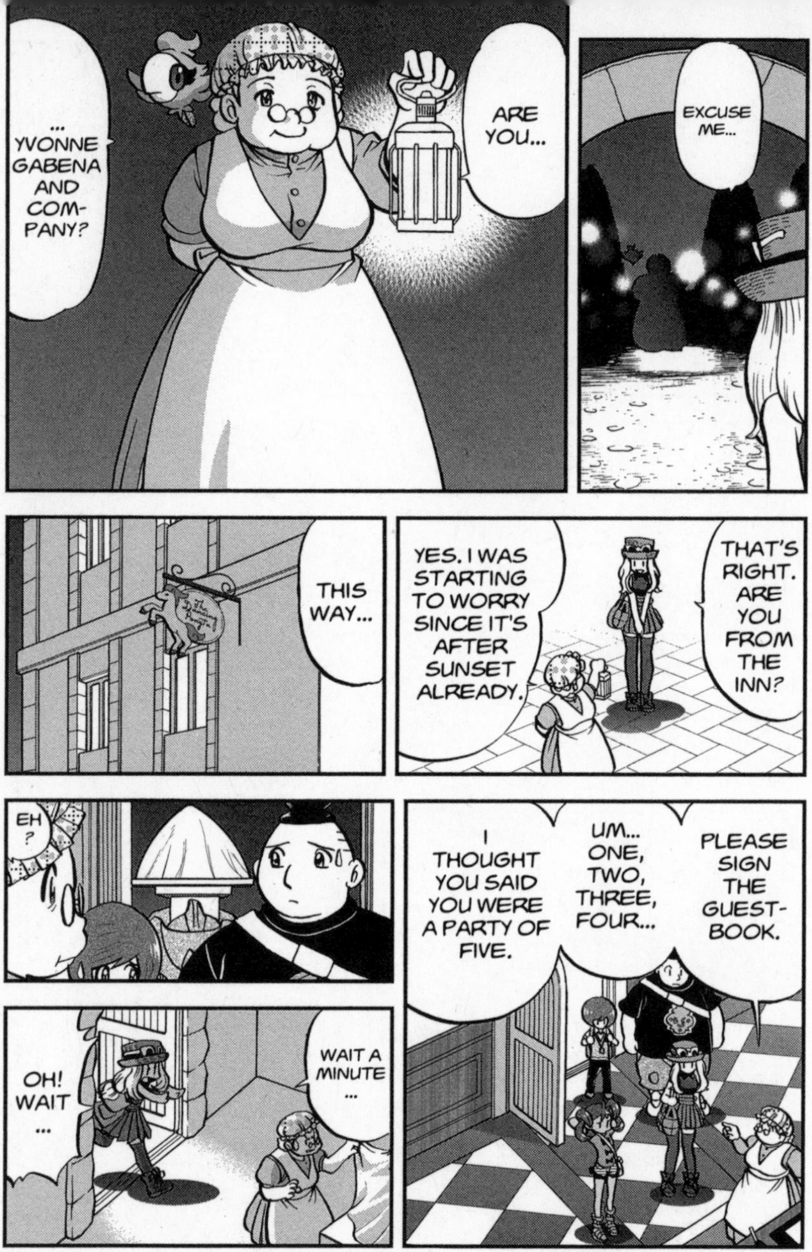
EXCUSE ME...
ARE YOU...
...YVONNE GABENA AND COMPANY?
THAT'S RIGHT. ARE YOU FROM THE INN?
YES. I WAS STARTING TO WORRY SINCE IT'S AFTER SUNSET ALREADY.
THIS WAY...
PLEASE SIGN THE GUEST-BOOK.
UM... ONE, TWO, THREE, FOUR...
I THOUGHT YOU SAID YOU WERE A PARTY OF FIVE.
EH?
WAIT A MINUTE...
OH! WAIT...

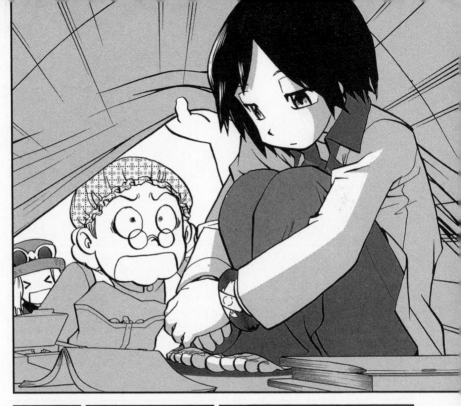

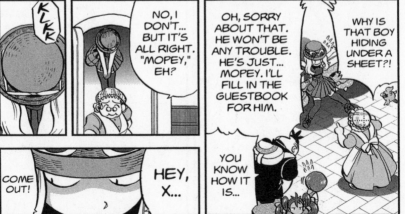

**KLKK**

NO, I DON'T... BUT IT'S ALL RIGHT. "MOPEY," EH?

OH, SORRY ABOUT THAT. HE WON'T BE ANY TROUBLE. HE'S JUST... MOPEY. I'LL FILL IN THE GUESTBOOK FOR HIM.

WHY IS THAT BOY HIDING UNDER A SHEET?!

YOU KNOW HOW IT IS...

COME OUT!

HEY, X...

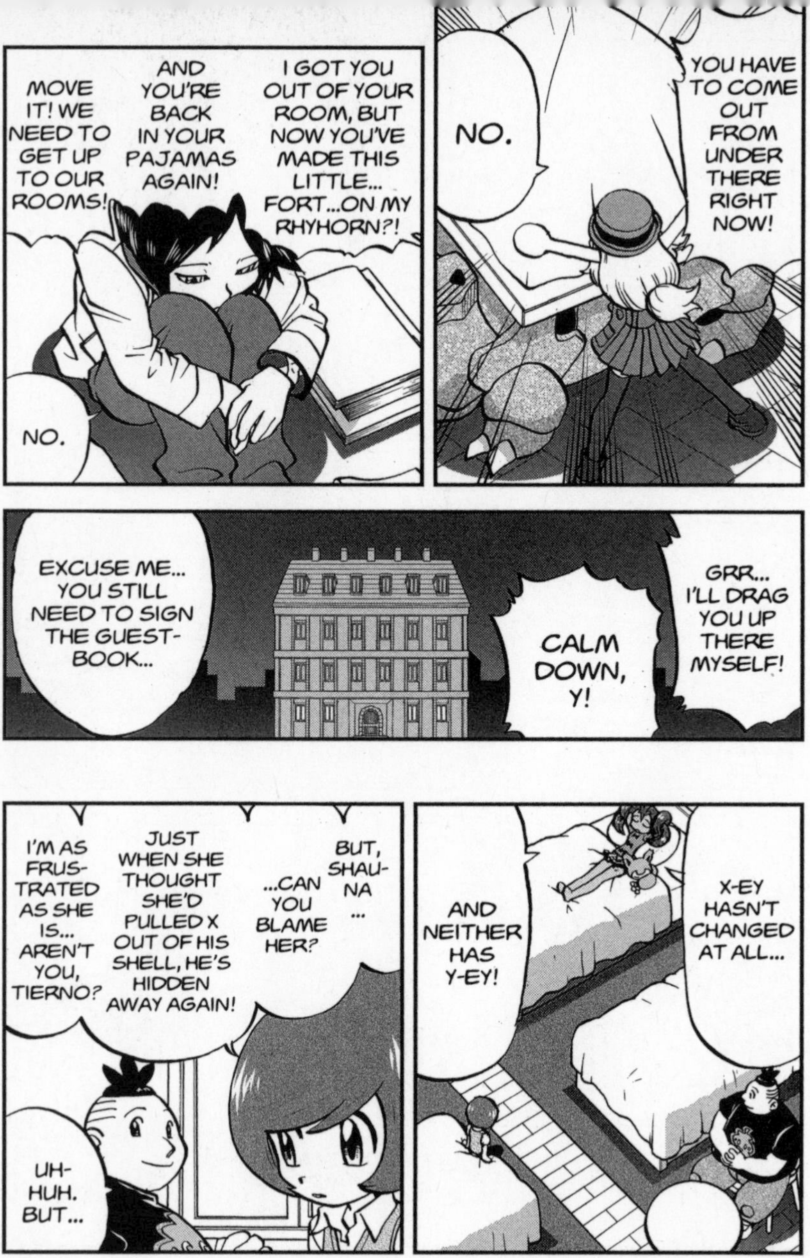
YOU HAVE TO COME OUT FROM UNDER THERE RIGHT NOW!
NO.
I GOT YOU OUT OF YOUR ROOM, BUT NOW YOU'VE MADE THIS LITTLE... FORT...ON MY RHYHORN?!
AND YOU'RE BACK IN YOUR PAJAMAS AGAIN!
MOVE IT! WE NEED TO GET UP TO OUR ROOMS!
NO.
GRR... I'LL DRAG YOU UP THERE MYSELF!
CALM DOWN, Y!
EXCUSE ME... YOU STILL NEED TO SIGN THE GUEST-BOOK...
X-EY HASN'T CHANGED AT ALL...
AND NEITHER HAS Y-EY!
BUT, SHAU-NA ...
...CAN YOU BLAME HER?
JUST WHEN SHE THOUGHT SHE'D PULLED X OUT OF HIS SHELL, HE'S HIDDEN AWAY AGAIN!
I'M AS FRUS-TRATED AS SHE IS... AREN'T YOU, TIERNO?
UH-HUH. BUT...

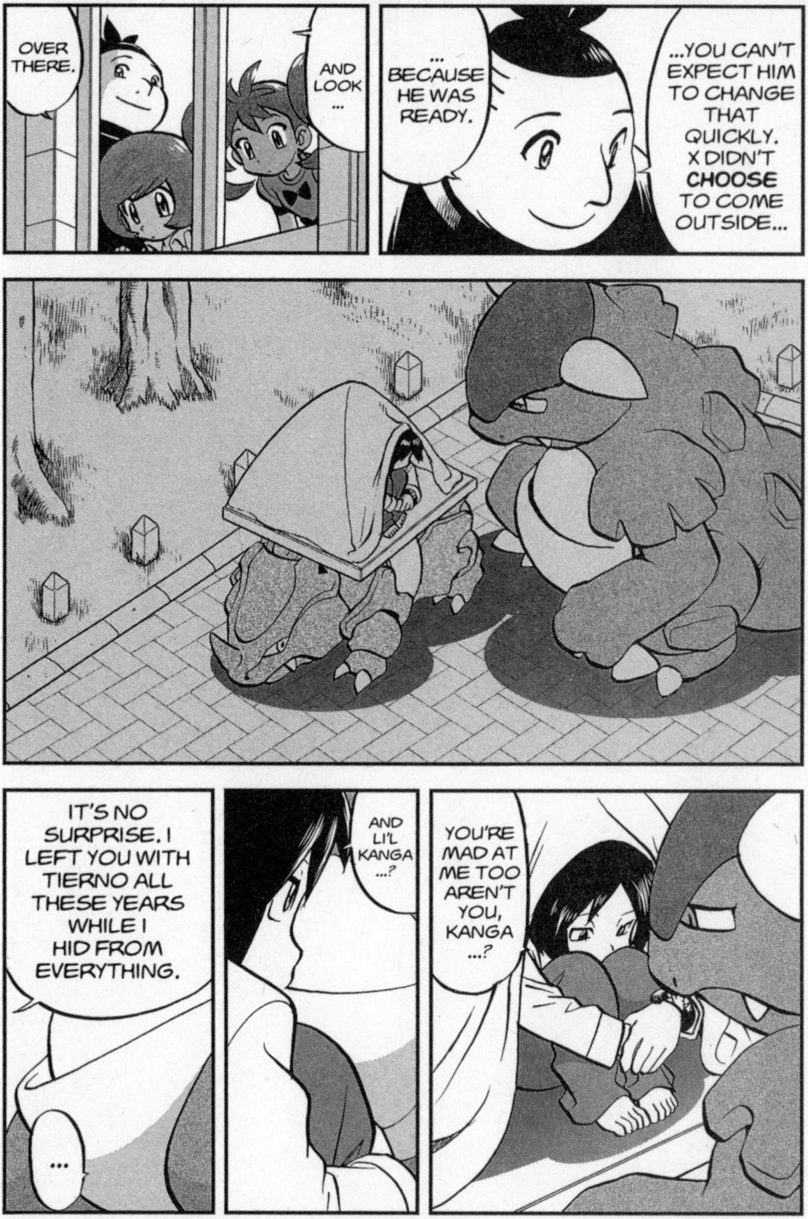

...YOU CAN'T EXPECT HIM TO CHANGE THAT QUICKLY. X DIDN'T **CHOOSE** TO COME OUTSIDE...
... BECAUSE HE WAS READY.
AND LOOK ...
OVER THERE.
YOU'RE MAD AT ME TOO AREN'T YOU, KANGA ...?
AND LI'L KANGA ...?
IT'S NO SURPRISE. I LEFT YOU WITH TIERNO ALL THESE YEARS WHILE I HID FROM EVERYTHING.
...

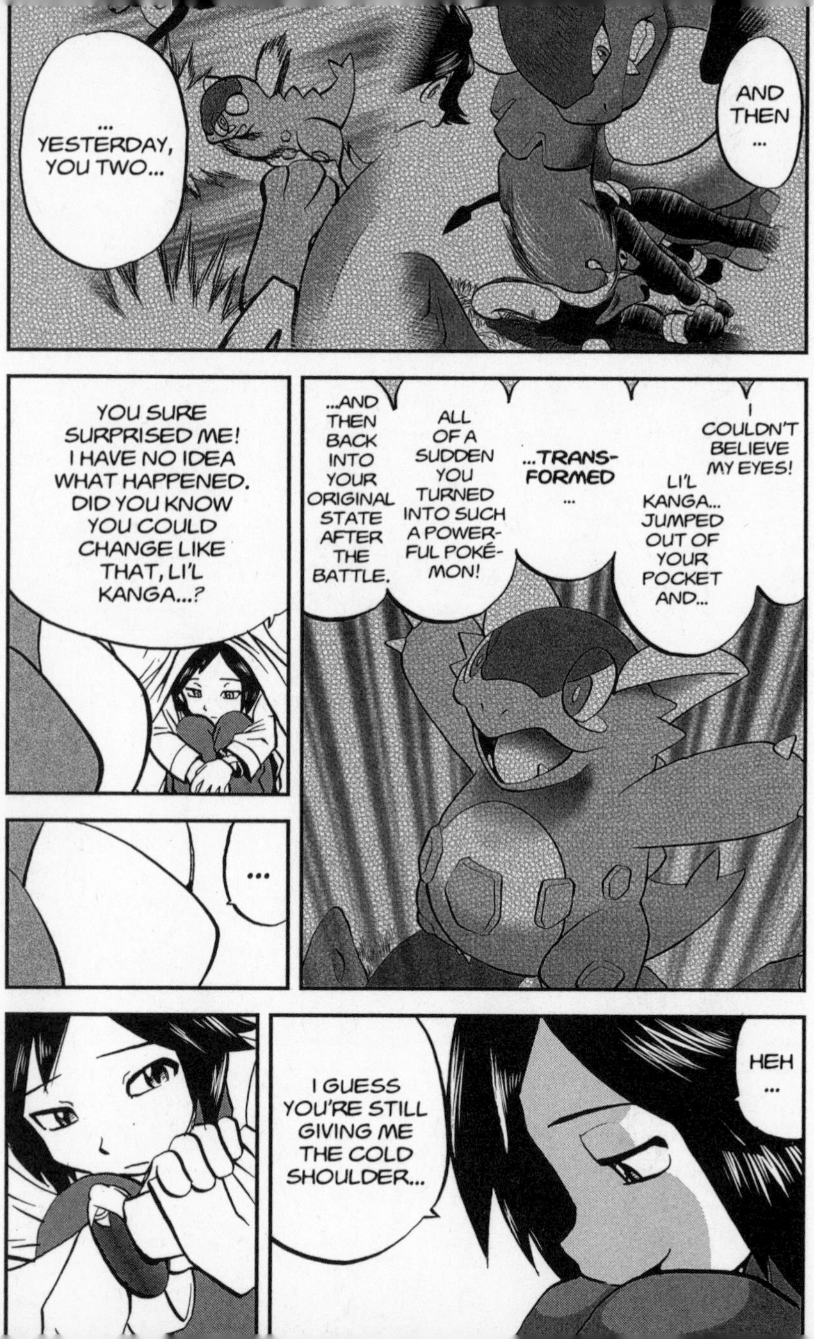
AND THEN ...
... YESTERDAY, YOU TWO...
I COULDN'T BELIEVE MY EYES!
LI'L KANGA... JUMPED OUT OF YOUR POCKET AND...
...TRANSFORMED ...
ALL OF A SUDDEN YOU TURNED INTO SUCH A POWERFUL POKÉMON!
...AND THEN BACK INTO YOUR ORIGINAL STATE AFTER THE BATTLE.
YOU SURE SURPRISED ME! I HAVE NO IDEA WHAT HAPPENED. DID YOU KNOW YOU COULD CHANGE LIKE THAT, LI'L KANGA...?
...
HEH ...
I GUESS YOU'RE STILL GIVING ME THE COLD SHOULDER...

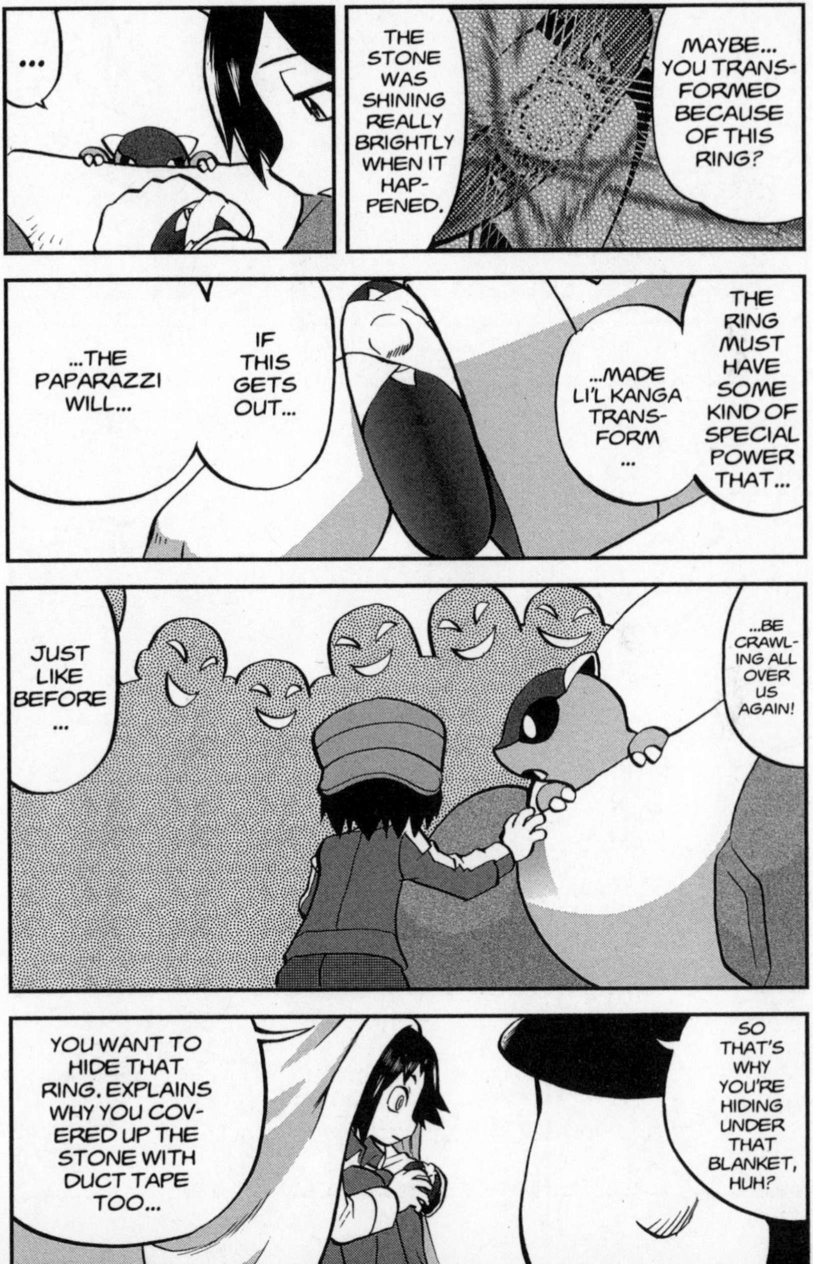
MAYBE... YOU TRANSFORMED BECAUSE OF THIS RING?
THE STONE WAS SHINING REALLY BRIGHTLY WHEN IT HAPPENED.
...
THE RING MUST HAVE SOME KIND OF SPECIAL POWER THAT...
...MADE LI'L KANGA TRANSFORM...
IF THIS GETS OUT...
...THE PAPARAZZI WILL...
...BE CRAWLING ALL OVER US AGAIN!
JUST LIKE BEFORE...
SO THAT'S WHY YOU'RE HIDING UNDER THAT BLANKET, HUH?
YOU WANT TO HIDE THAT RING. EXPLAINS WHY YOU COVERED UP THE STONE WITH DUCT TAPE TOO...

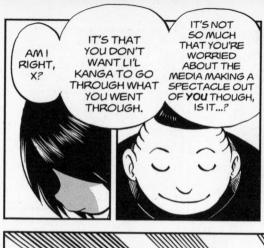

FLAP FLAP FLAP
IT'S NOT SO MUCH THAT YOU'RE WORRIED ABOUT THE MEDIA MAKING A SPECTACLE OUT OF **YOU** THOUGH, IS IT...?
IT'S THAT YOU DON'T WANT LI'L KANGA TO GO THROUGH WHAT YOU WENT THROUGH.
AM I RIGHT, X?
BOM
BOM BOM
WHO ARE THOSE TWO...?
CHES-PIN ...
...AND FROAKIE.

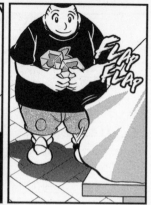

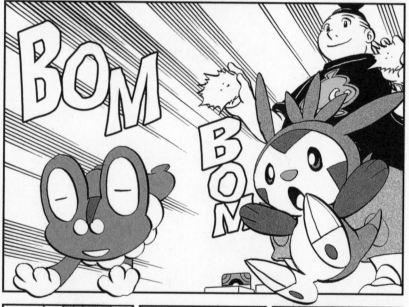

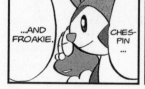

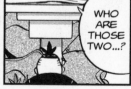

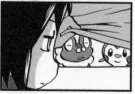

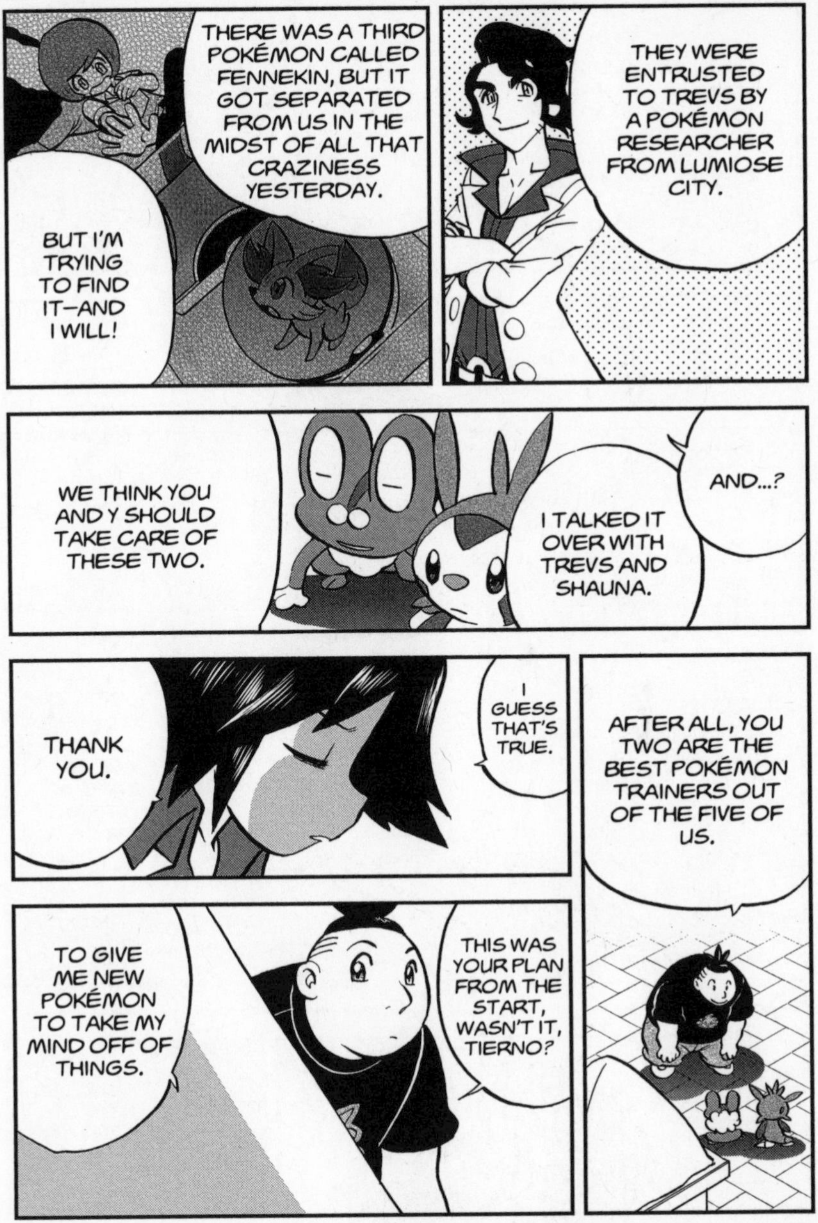
THEY WERE ENTRUSTED TO TREVS BY A POKÉMON RESEARCHER FROM LUMIOSE CITY.
THERE WAS A THIRD POKÉMON CALLED FENNEKIN, BUT IT GOT SEPARATED FROM US IN THE MIDST OF ALL THAT CRAZINESS YESTERDAY.
BUT I'M TRYING TO FIND IT—AND I WILL!
AND...?
I TALKED IT OVER WITH TREVS AND SHAUNA.
WE THINK YOU AND Y SHOULD TAKE CARE OF THESE TWO.
AFTER ALL, YOU TWO ARE THE BEST POKÉMON TRAINERS OUT OF THE FIVE OF US.
I GUESS THAT'S TRUE.
THANK YOU.
THIS WAS YOUR PLAN FROM THE START, WASN'T IT, TIERNO?
TO GIVE ME NEW POKÉMON TO TAKE MY MIND OFF OF THINGS.

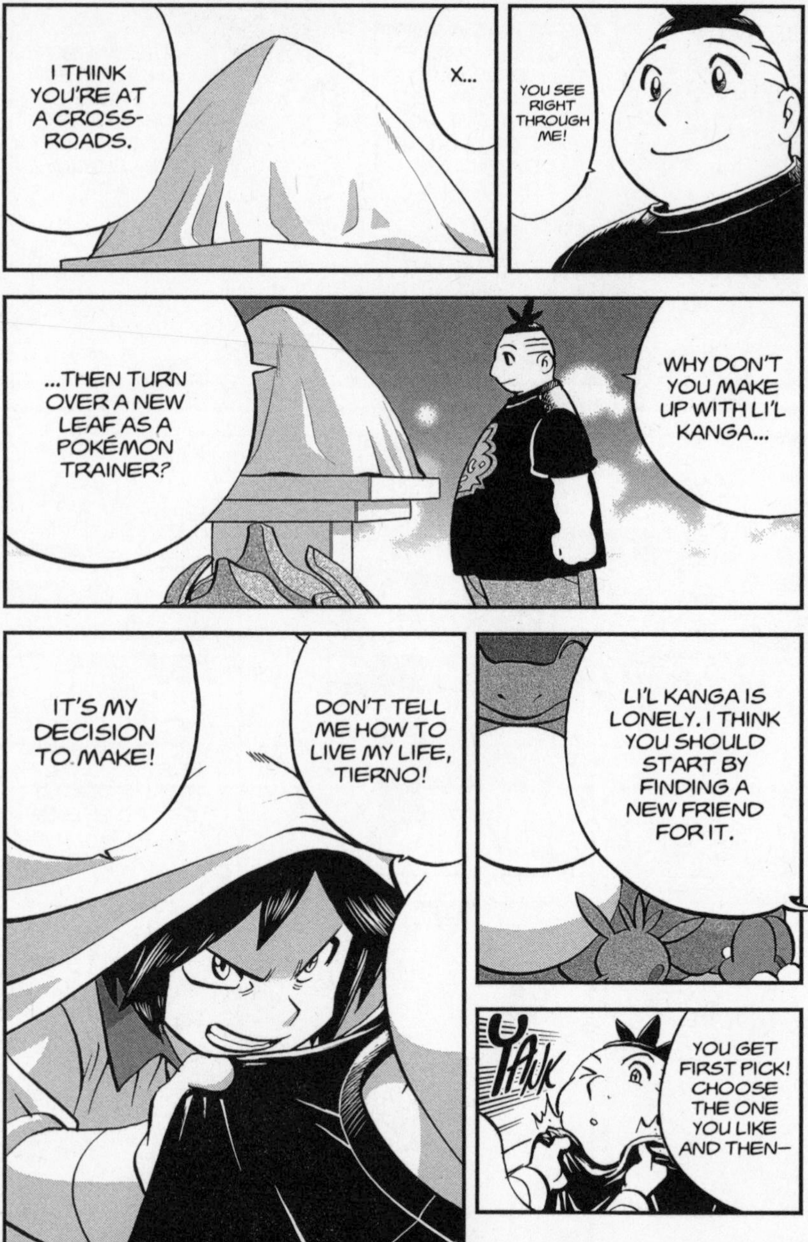
X...
YOU SEE RIGHT THROUGH ME!
I THINK YOU'RE AT A CROSS-ROADS.
WHY DON'T YOU MAKE UP WITH LI'L KANGA...
...THEN TURN OVER A NEW LEAF AS A POKÉMON TRAINER?
LI'L KANGA IS LONELY. I THINK YOU SHOULD START BY FINDING A NEW FRIEND FOR IT.
YOU GET FIRST PICK! CHOOSE THE ONE YOU LIKE AND THEN—
YANK
DON'T TELL ME HOW TO LIVE MY LIFE, TIERNO!
IT'S MY DECISION TO MAKE!

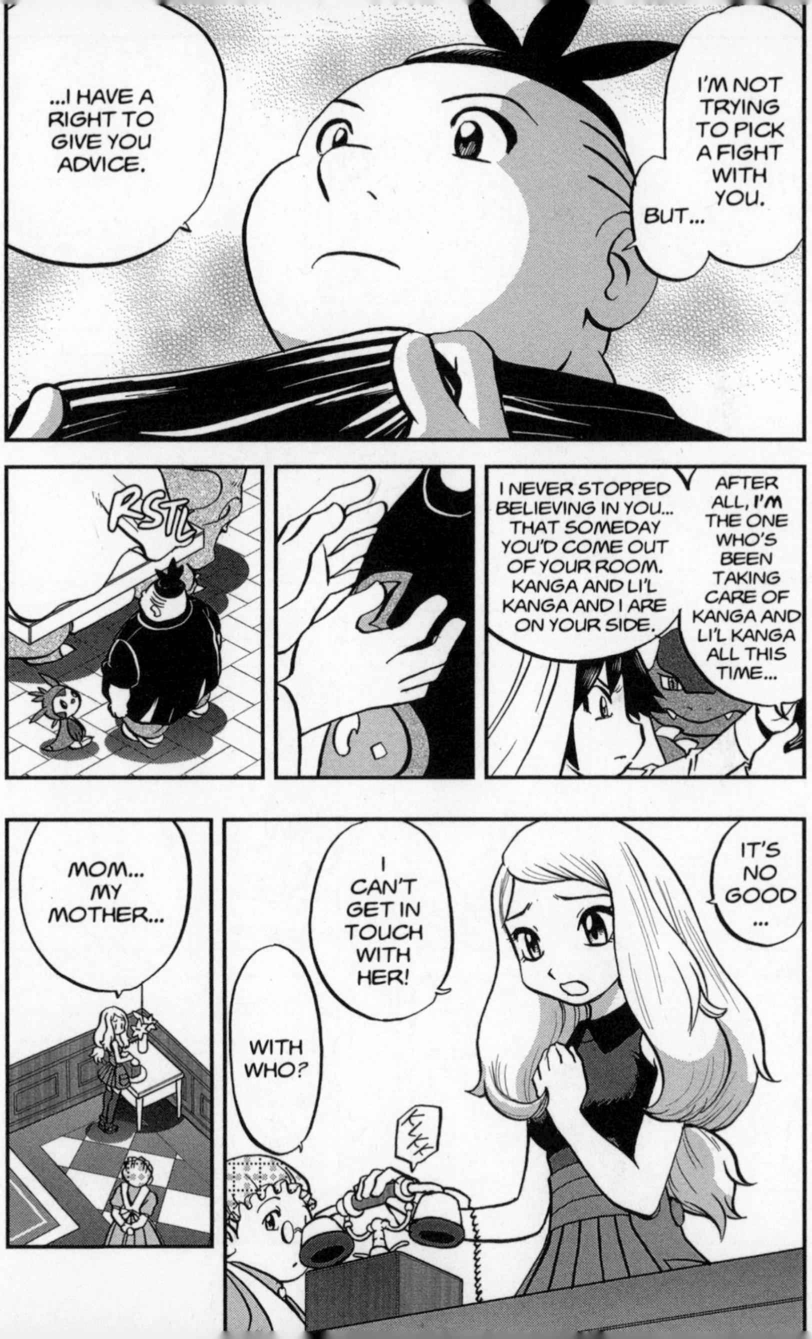
I'M NOT TRYING TO PICK A FIGHT WITH YOU.
BUT...
...I HAVE A RIGHT TO GIVE YOU ADVICE.
AFTER ALL, I'M THE ONE WHO'S BEEN TAKING CARE OF KANGA AND LI'L KANGA ALL THIS TIME...
I NEVER STOPPED BELIEVING IN YOU... THAT SOMEDAY YOU'D COME OUT OF YOUR ROOM. KANGA AND LI'L KANGA AND I ARE ON YOUR SIDE.
RSTL
IT'S NO GOOD...
I CAN'T GET IN TOUCH WITH HER!
KLKK
WITH WHO?
MOM... MY MOTHER...

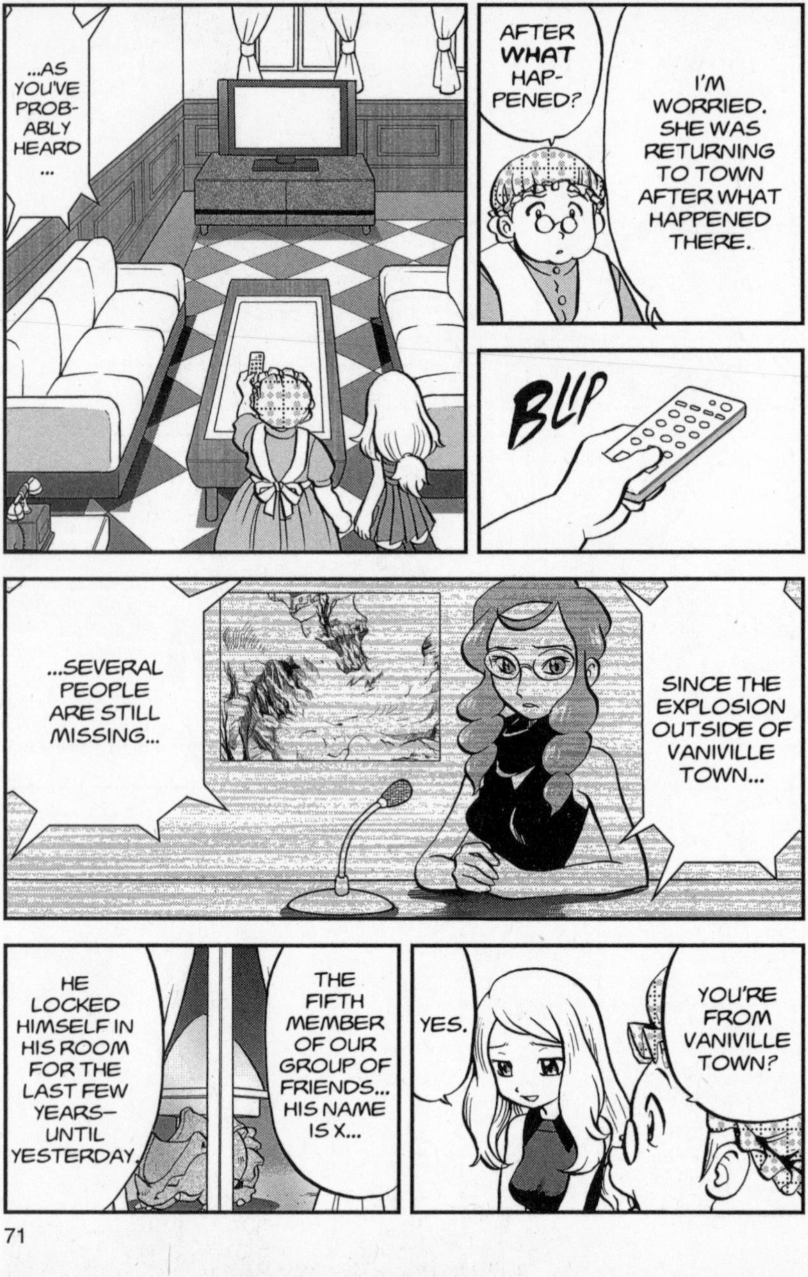
I'M WORRIED. SHE WAS RETURNING TO TOWN AFTER WHAT HAPPENED THERE.
AFTER WHAT HAP-PENED?
BLIP
...AS YOU'VE PROB-ABLY HEARD ...
SINCE THE EXPLOSION OUTSIDE OF VANIVILLE TOWN...
...SEVERAL PEOPLE ARE STILL MISSING...
YOU'RE FROM VANIVILLE TOWN?
YES.
THE FIFTH MEMBER OF OUR GROUP OF FRIENDS... HIS NAME IS X...
HE LOCKED HIMSELF IN HIS ROOM FOR THE LAST FEW YEARS—UNTIL YESTERDAY.

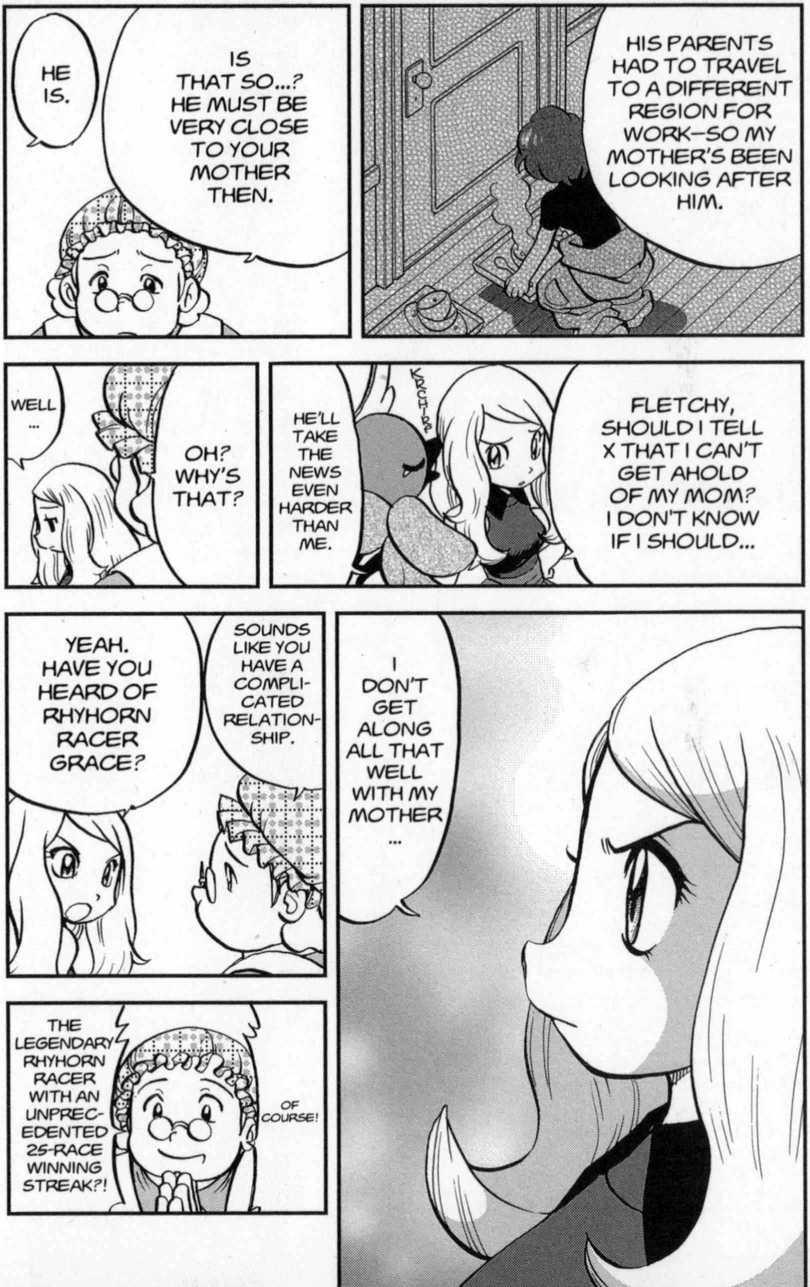
HIS PARENTS HAD TO TRAVEL TO A DIFFERENT REGION FOR WORK—SO MY MOTHER'S BEEN LOOKING AFTER HIM.
IS THAT SO...? HE MUST BE VERY CLOSE TO YOUR MOTHER THEN.
HE IS.
FLETCHY, SHOULD I TELL X THAT I CAN'T GET AHOLD OF MY MOM? I DON'T KNOW IF I SHOULD...
KRCHIRP
HE'LL TAKE THE NEWS EVEN HARDER THAN ME.
OH? WHY'S THAT?
WELL ...
I DON'T GET ALONG ALL THAT WELL WITH MY MOTHER ...
SOUNDS LIKE YOU HAVE A COMPLICATED RELATIONSHIP.
YEAH. HAVE YOU HEARD OF RHYHORN RACER GRACE?
OF COURSE!
THE LEGENDARY RHYHORN RACER WITH AN UNPRECEDENTED 25-RACE WINNING STREAK?!

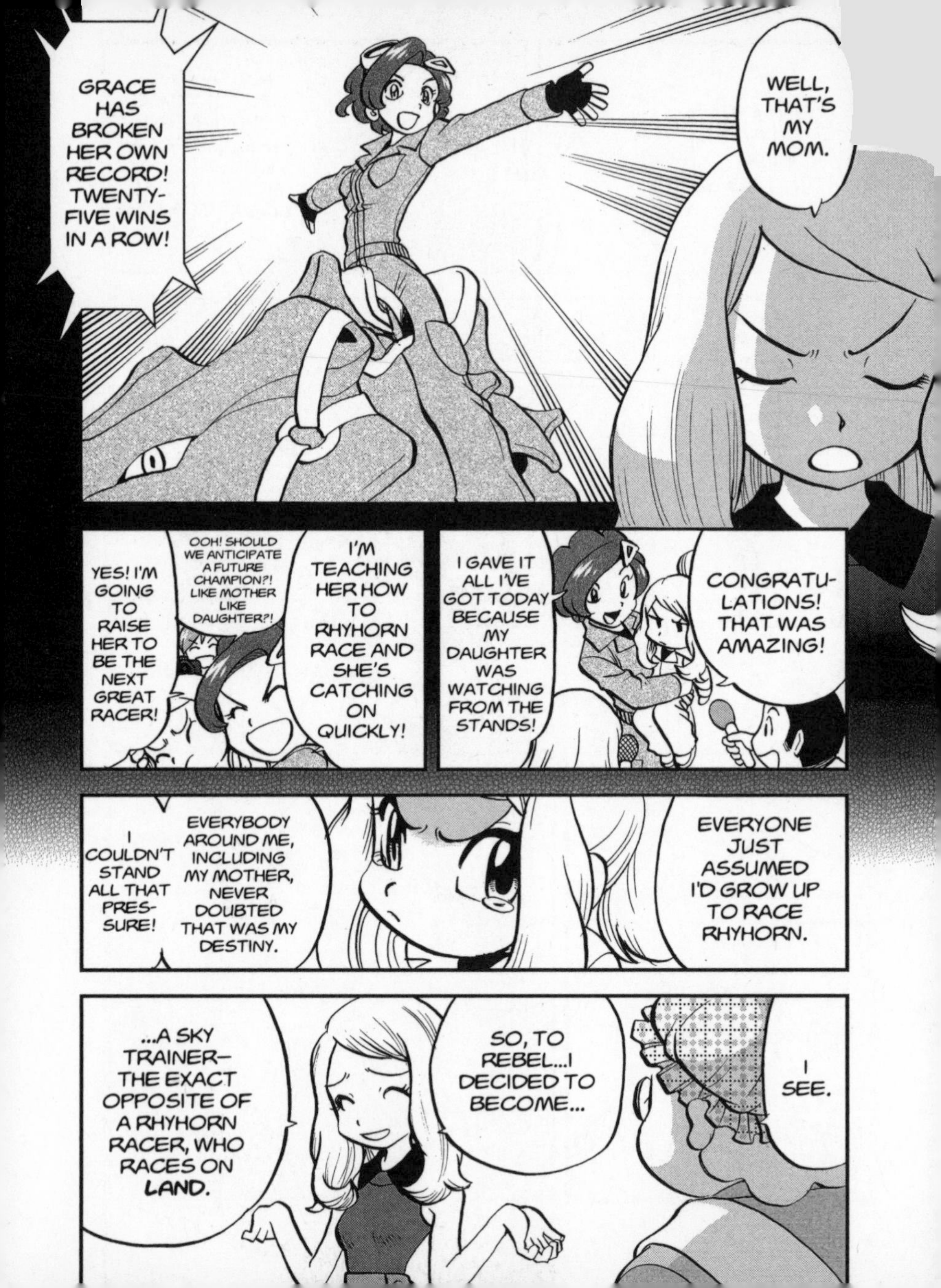
WELL, THAT'S MY MOM.
GRACE HAS BROKEN HER OWN RECORD! TWENTY-FIVE WINS IN A ROW!
CONGRATU-LATIONS! THAT WAS AMAZING!
I GAVE IT ALL I'VE GOT TODAY BECAUSE MY DAUGHTER WAS WATCHING FROM THE STANDS!
I'M TEACHING HER HOW TO RHYHORN RACE AND SHE'S CATCHING ON QUICKLY!
OOH! SHOULD WE ANTICIPATE A FUTURE CHAMPION?! LIKE MOTHER LIKE DAUGHTER?!
YES! I'M GOING TO RAISE HER TO BE THE NEXT GREAT RACER!
EVERYONE JUST ASSUMED I'D GROW UP TO RACE RHYHORN.
EVERYBODY AROUND ME, INCLUDING MY MOTHER, NEVER DOUBTED THAT WAS MY DESTINY.
I COULDN'T STAND ALL THAT PRES-SURE!
I SEE.
SO, TO REBEL...I DECIDED TO BECOME...
...A SKY TRAINER—THE EXACT OPPOSITE OF A RHYHORN RACER, WHO RACES ON **LAND**.

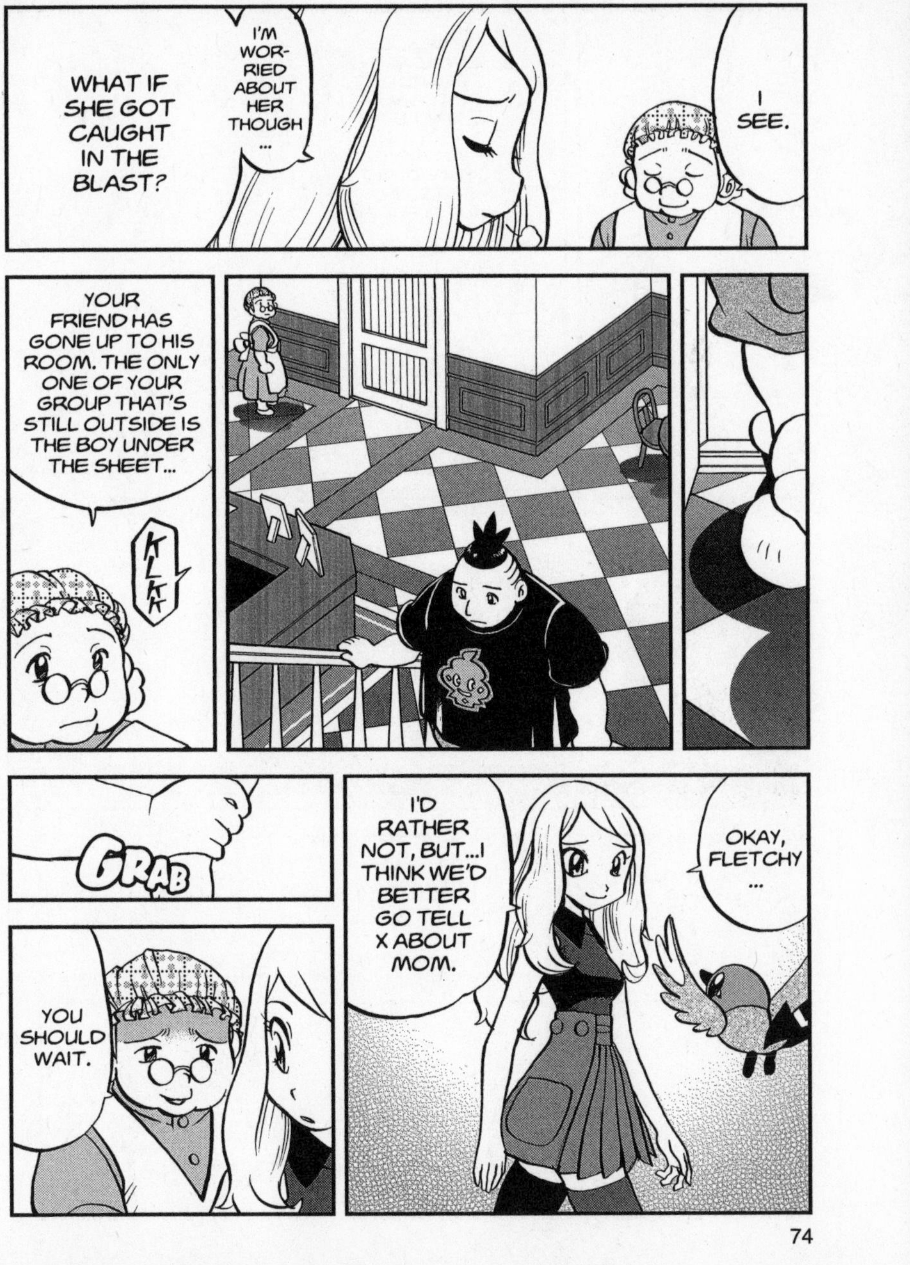
I SEE.
I'M WORRIED ABOUT HER THOUGH...
WHAT IF SHE GOT CAUGHT IN THE BLAST?
YOUR FRIEND HAS GONE UP TO HIS ROOM. THE ONLY ONE OF YOUR GROUP THAT'S STILL OUTSIDE IS THE BOY UNDER THE SHEET...
KLKK
OKAY, FLETCHY...
I'D RATHER NOT, BUT...I THINK WE'D BETTER GO TELL X ABOUT MOM.
GRAB
YOU SHOULD WAIT.

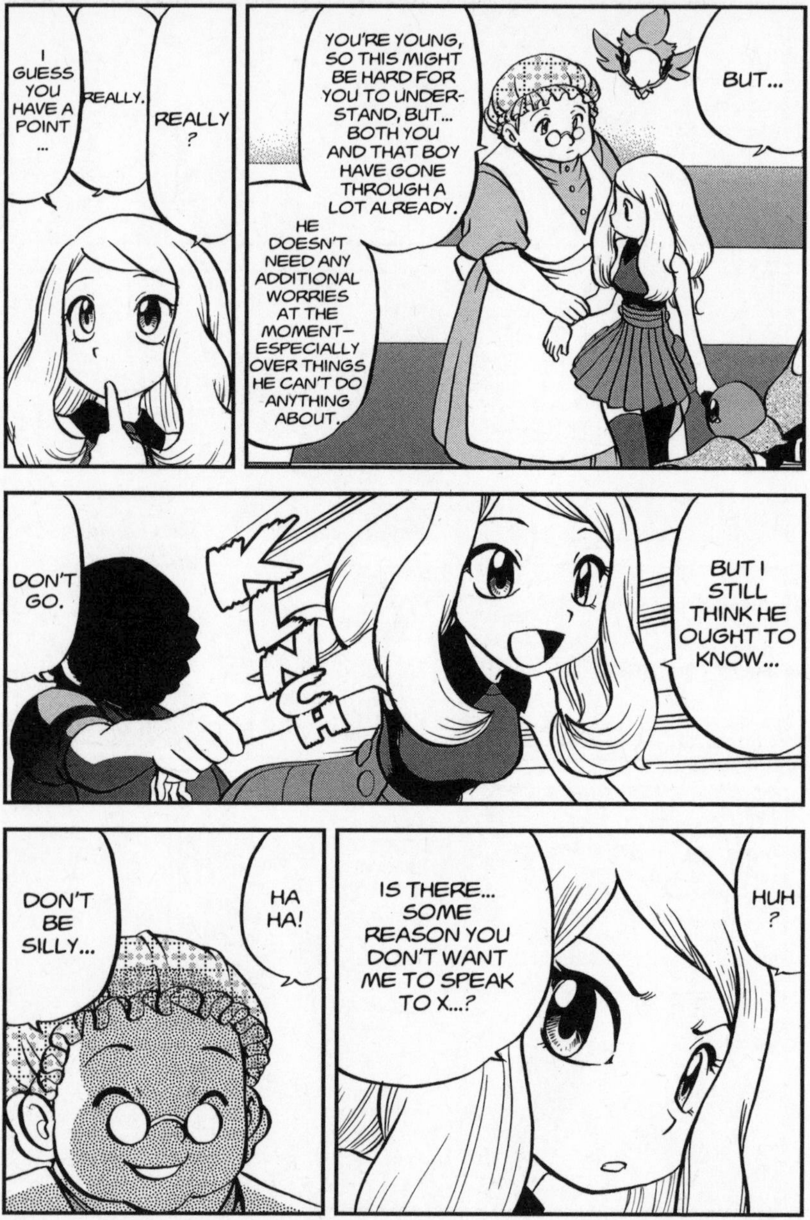
BUT...
YOU'RE YOUNG, SO THIS MIGHT BE HARD FOR YOU TO UNDER-STAND, BUT... BOTH YOU AND THAT BOY HAVE GONE THROUGH A LOT ALREADY.
HE DOESN'T NEED ANY ADDITIONAL WORRIES AT THE MOMENT— ESPECIALLY OVER THINGS HE CAN'T DO ANYTHING ABOUT.
REALLY?
REALLY.
I GUESS YOU HAVE A POINT...
BUT I STILL THINK HE OUGHT TO KNOW...
DON'T GO.
HUH?
IS THERE... SOME REASON YOU DON'T WANT ME TO SPEAK TO X...?
HA HA!
DON'T BE SILLY...

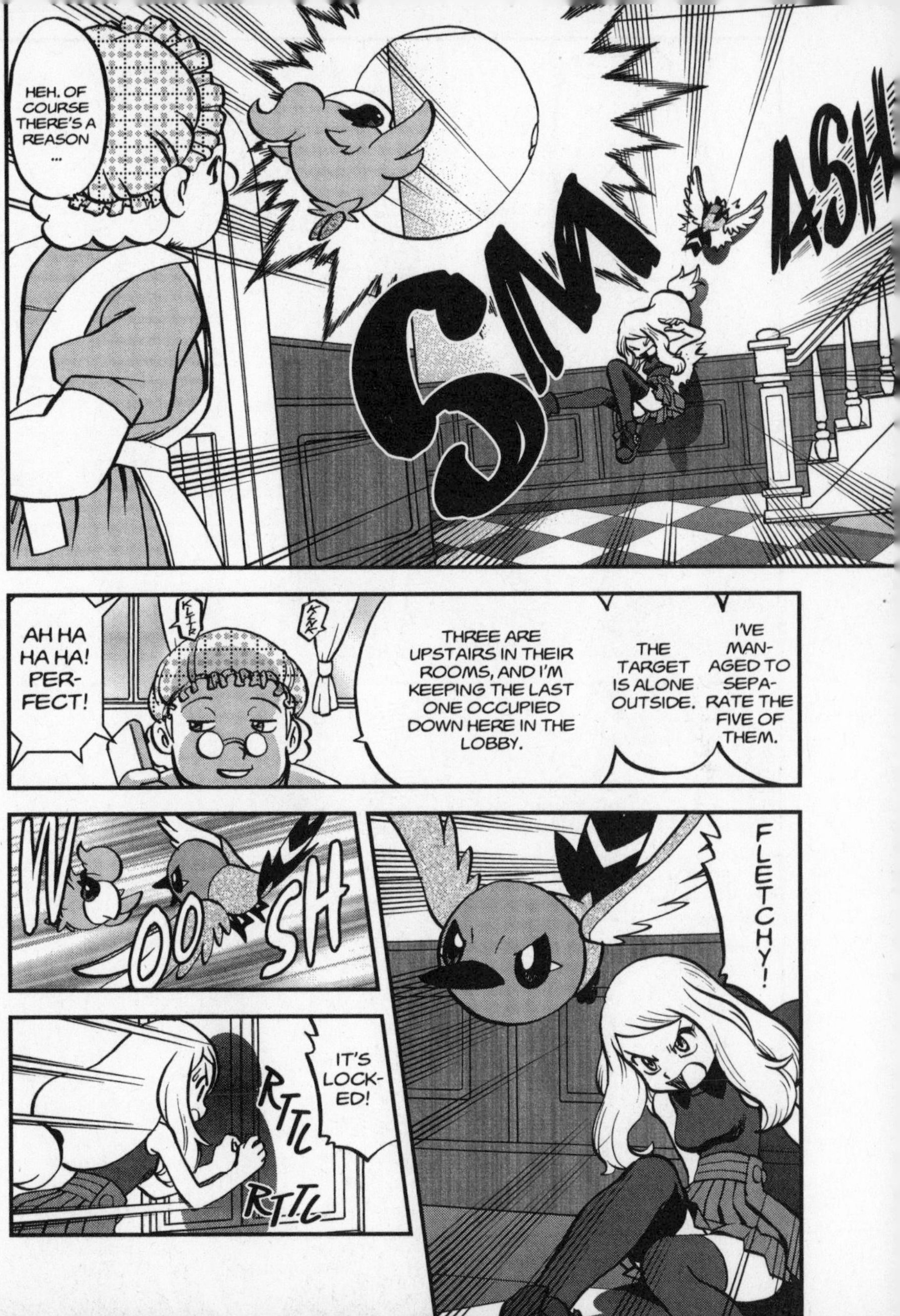
SMASH
HEH. OF COURSE THERE'S A REASON ...
I'VE MAN-AGED TO SEPA-RATE THE FIVE OF THEM.
THE TARGET IS ALONE OUTSIDE.
THREE ARE UPSTAIRS IN THEIR ROOMS, AND I'M KEEPING THE LAST ONE OCCUPIED DOWN HERE IN THE LOBBY.
KAK
KLTK
AH HA HA HA! PER-FECT!
FLETCHY!
WOOSH
IT'S LOCK-ED!
RTTL
RTTL

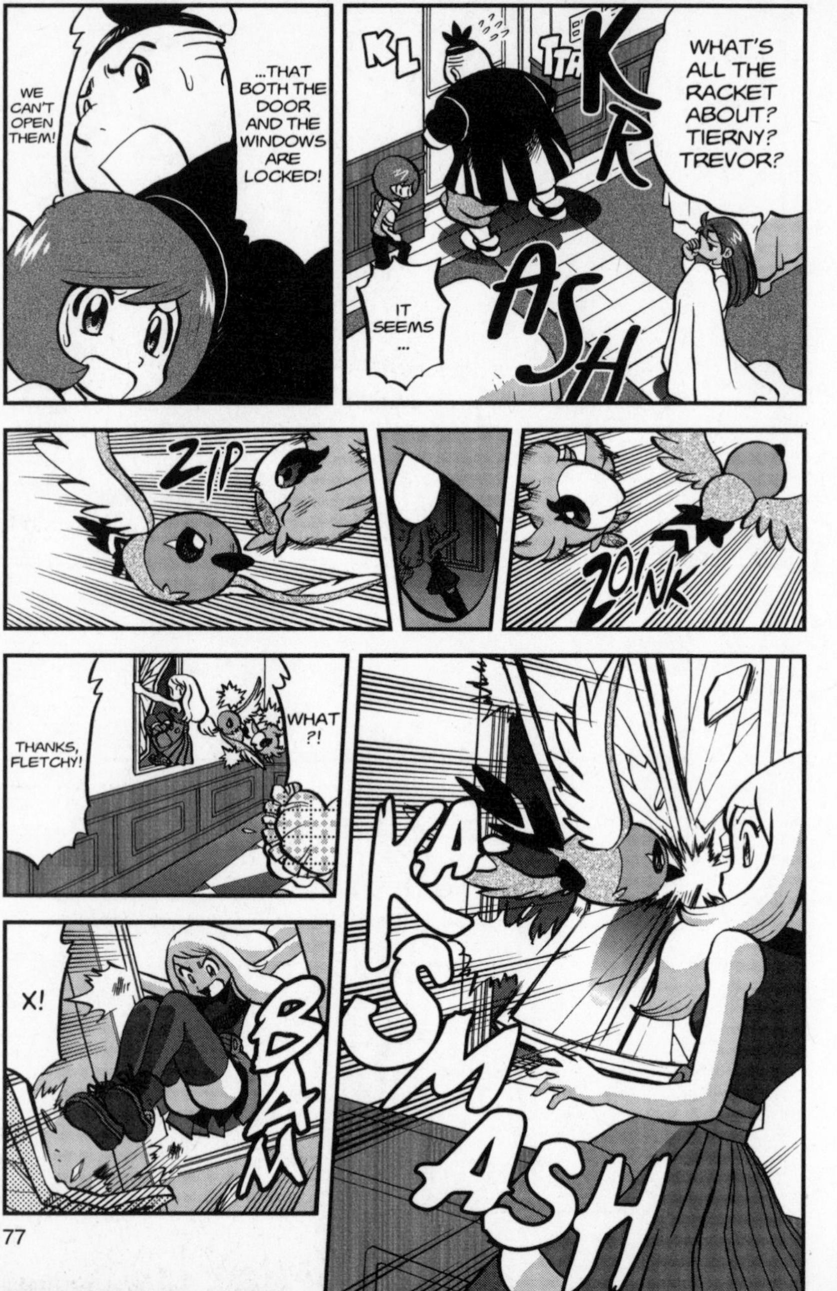
KL TTAKRASH
WHAT'S ALL THE RACKET ABOUT? TIERNY? TREVOR?
IT SEEMS ...
...THAT BOTH THE DOOR AND THE WINDOWS ARE LOCKED!
WE CAN'T OPEN THEM!
ZOINK
ZIP
KA-SMASH
WHAT ?!
THANKS, FLETCHY!
BAM
X!

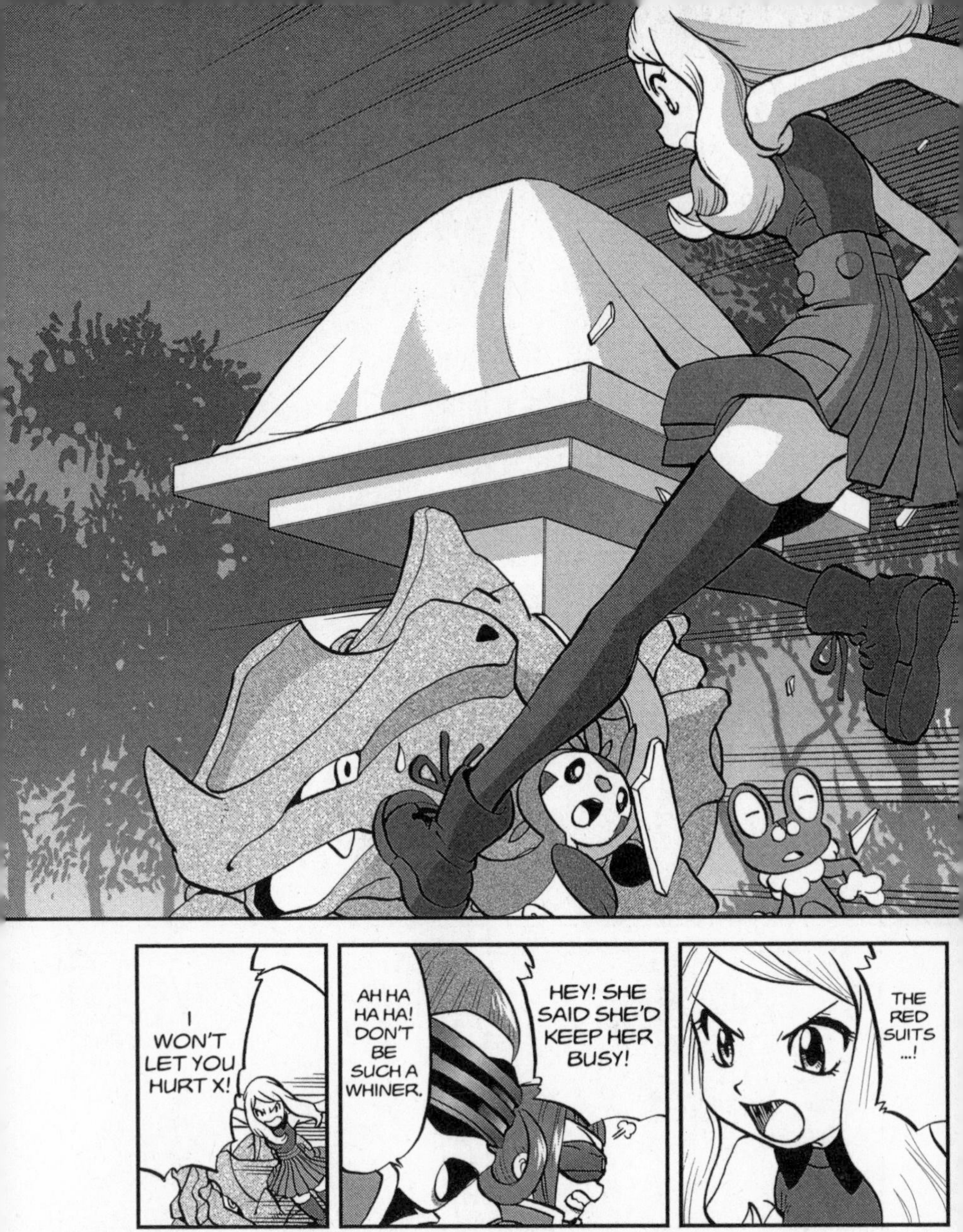
THE RED SUITS ...!
HEY! SHE SAID SHE'D KEEP HER BUSY!
AH HA HA HA! DON'T BE SUCH A WHINER.
I WON'T LET YOU HURT X!

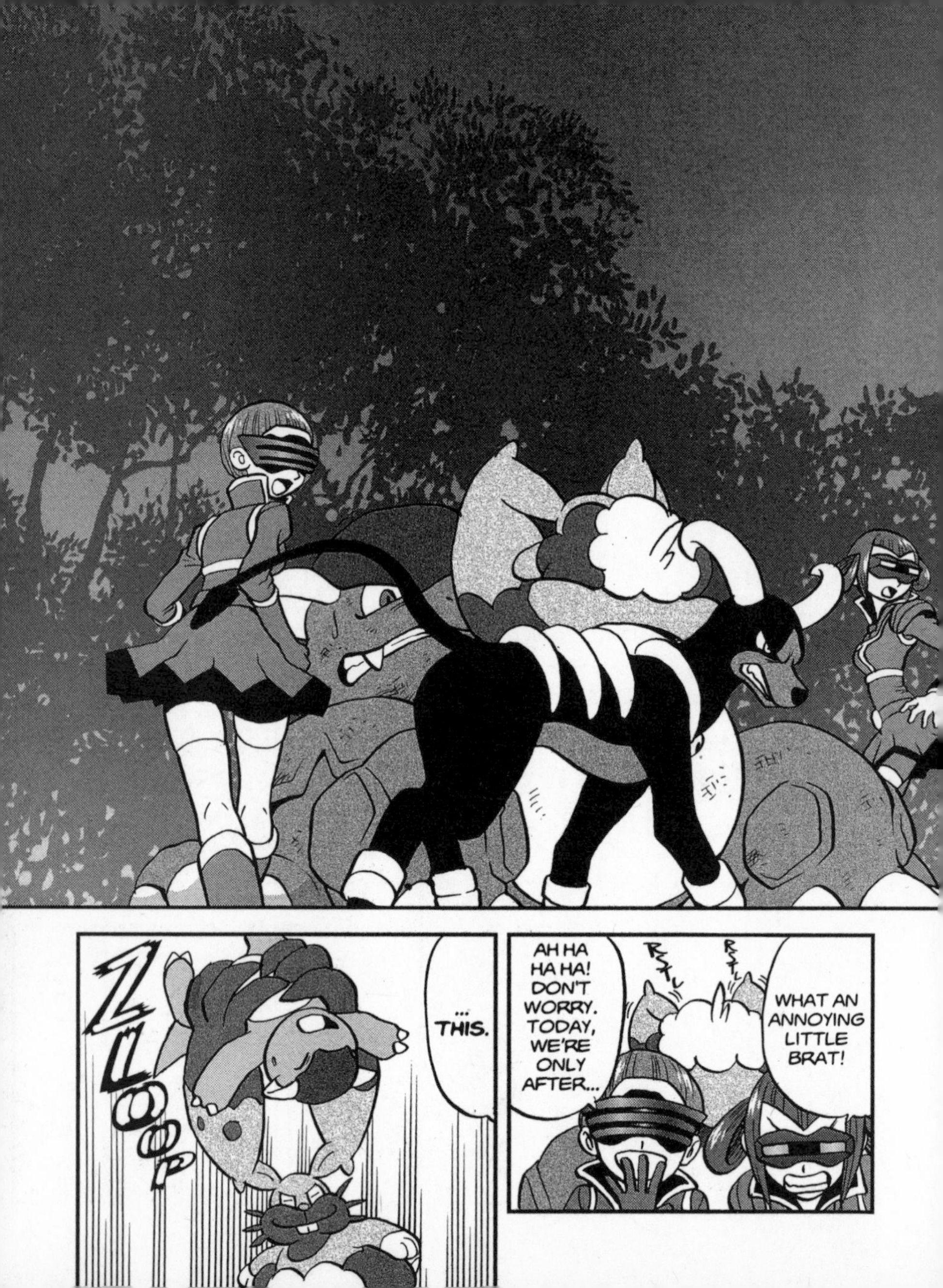
WHAT AN ANNOYING LITTLE BRAT!
RSTL
RSTL
AH HA HA HA! DON'T WORRY. TODAY, WE'RE ONLY AFTER...
...THIS.
ZUOOP

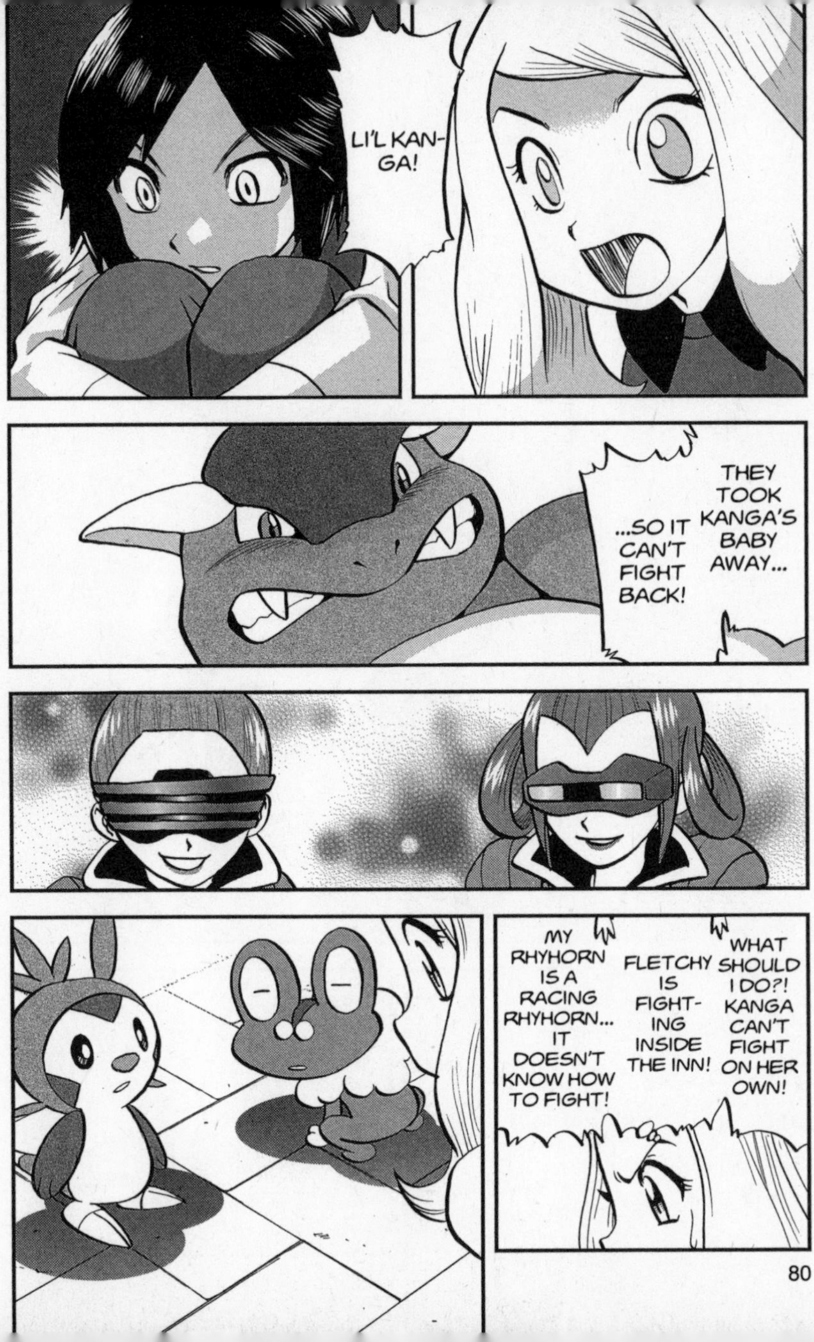
LI'L KANGA!
THEY TOOK KANGA'S BABY AWAY...
...SO IT CAN'T FIGHT BACK!
WHAT SHOULD I DO?! KANGA CAN'T FIGHT ON HER OWN!
FLETCHY IS FIGHTING INSIDE THE INN!
MY RHYHORN IS A RACING RHYHORN... IT DOESN'T KNOW HOW TO FIGHT!

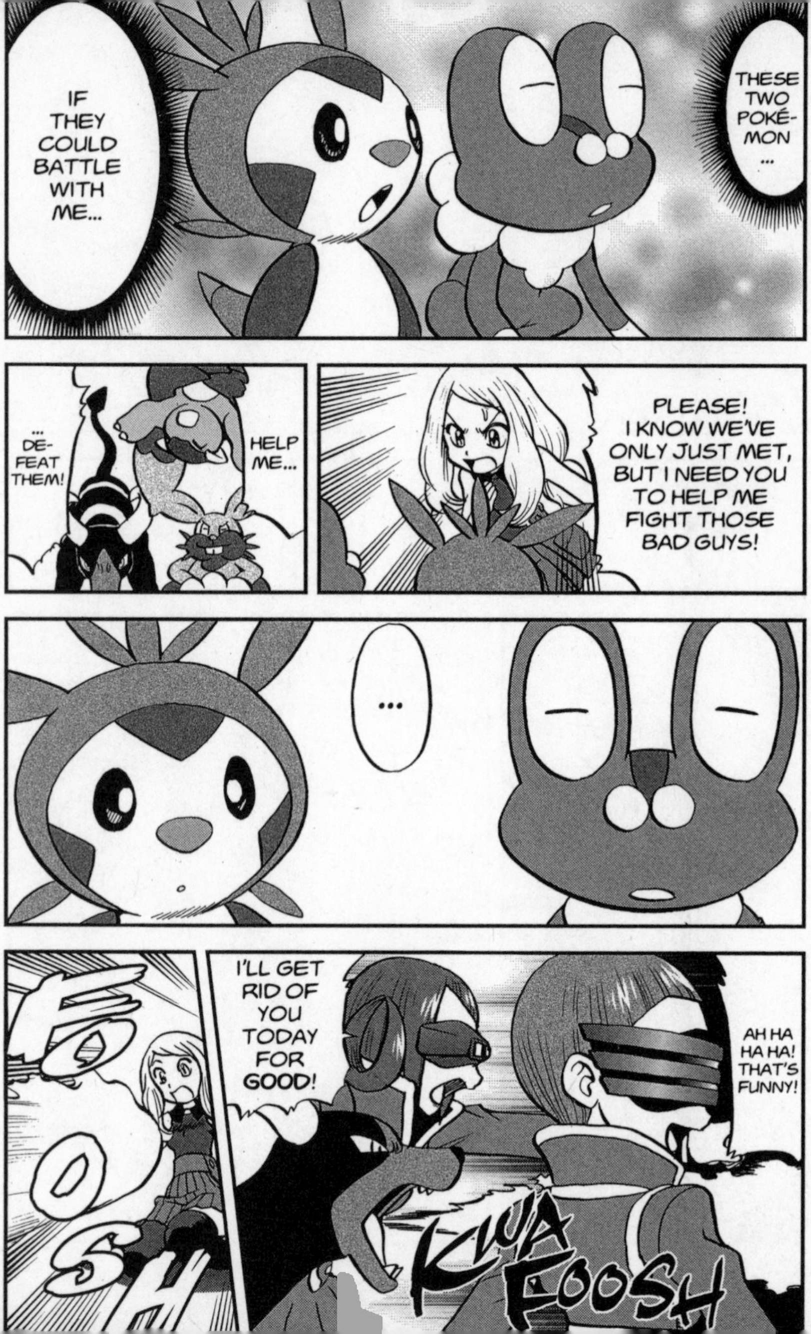
THESE TWO POKÉ-MON ...
IF THEY COULD BATTLE WITH ME...
PLEASE! I KNOW WE'VE ONLY JUST MET, BUT I NEED YOU TO HELP ME FIGHT THOSE BAD GUYS!
HELP ME...
... DE-FEAT THEM!
...
AH HA HA HA! THAT'S FUNNY!
I'LL GET RID OF YOU TODAY FOR GOOD!
KWA FOOSH
FOOSH

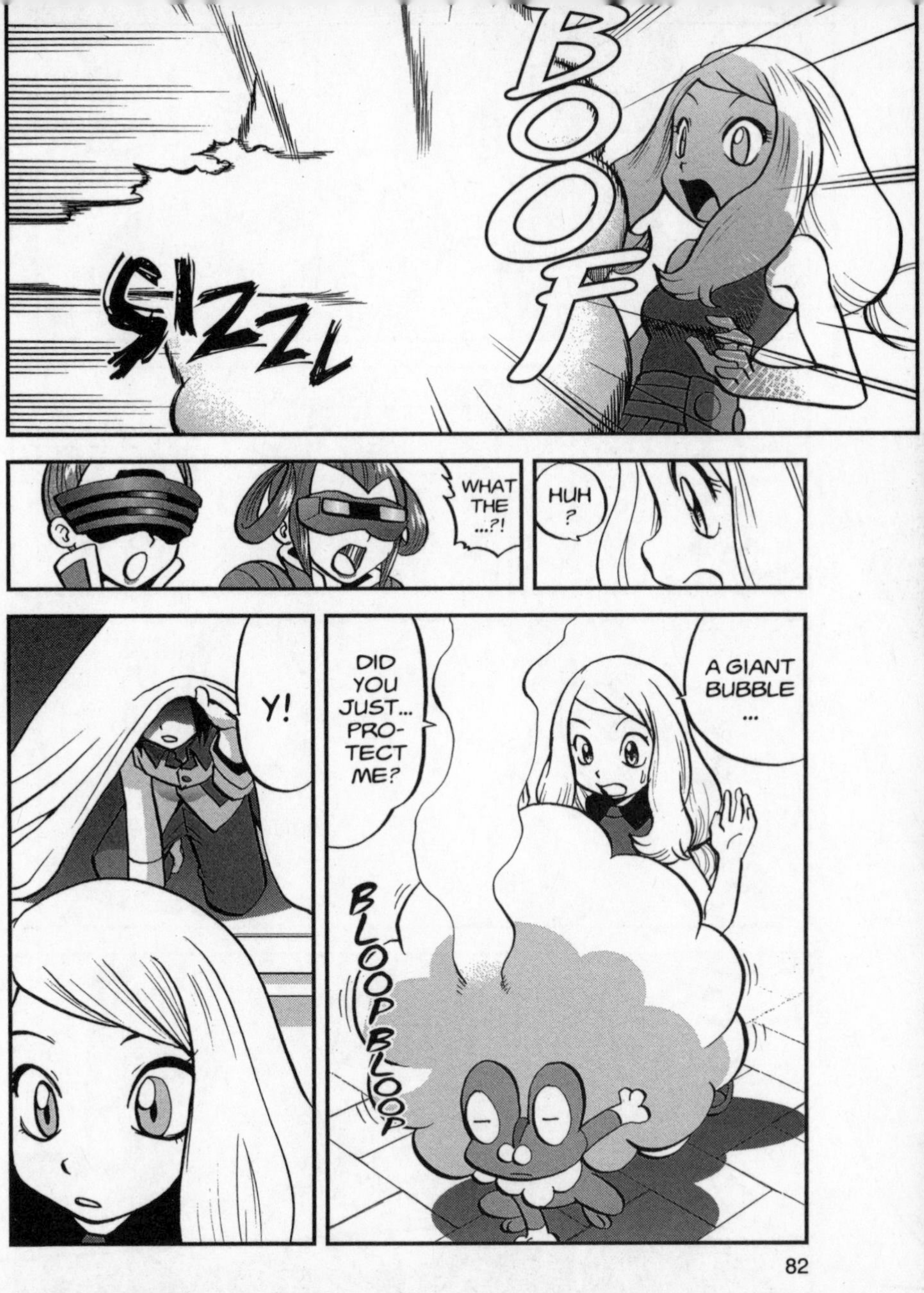
BOOF
SIZZL
HUH?
WHAT THE ...?!
A GIANT BUBBLE ...
DID YOU JUST... PRO-TECT ME?
BLOOPBLOOPBLOOP
Y!

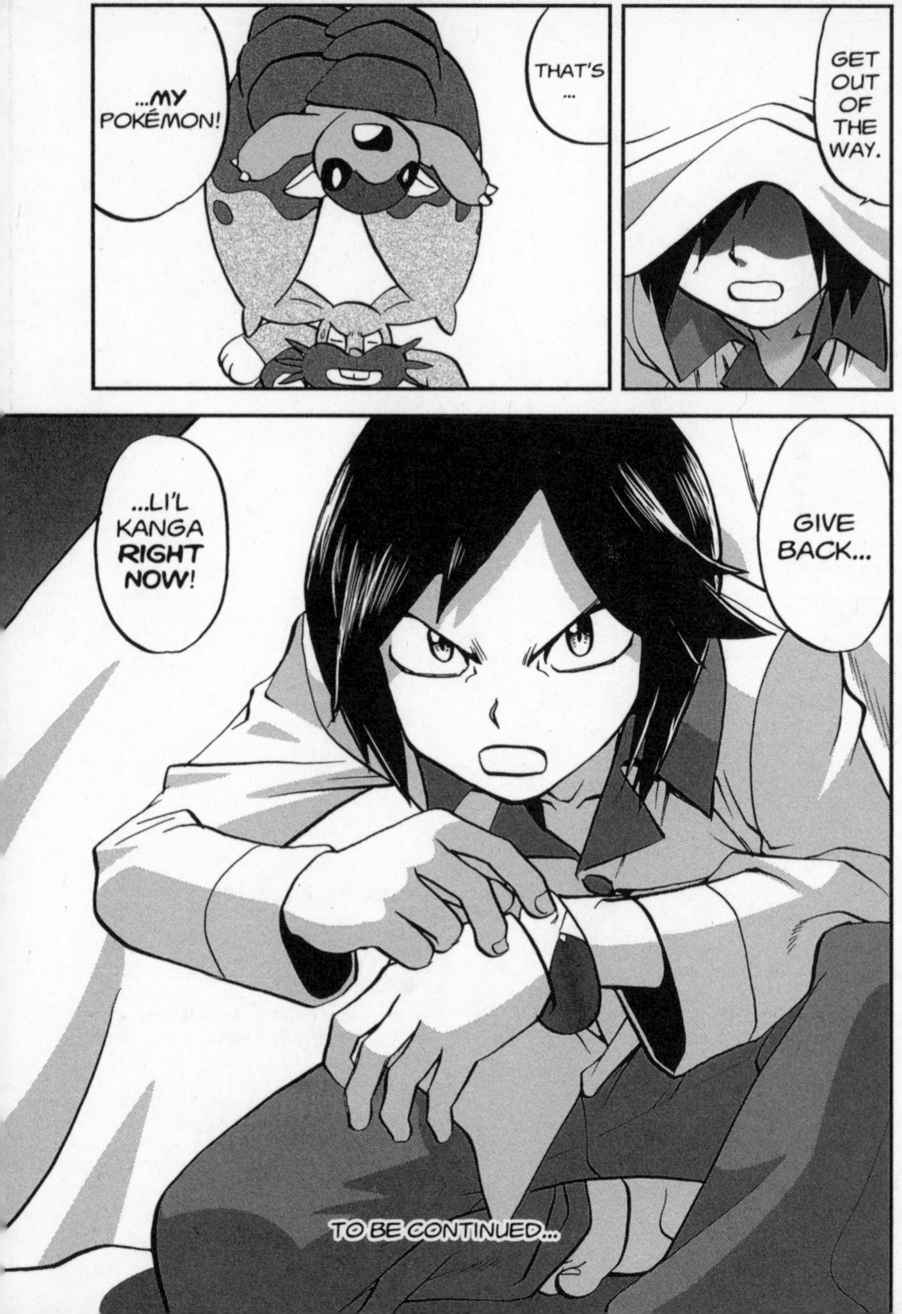
GET OUT OF THE WAY.
THAT'S ...
...MY POKÉMON!
GIVE BACK...
...LI'L KANGA RIGHT NOW!
TO BE CONTINUED...

## Current Location

**Route 1**
Vaniville Pathway

A small and quiet country lane that connects Vaniville Town and Aquacorde Town.

Aquacorde Town

A town that naturally sprang up as people flocked to this pristine riverside.

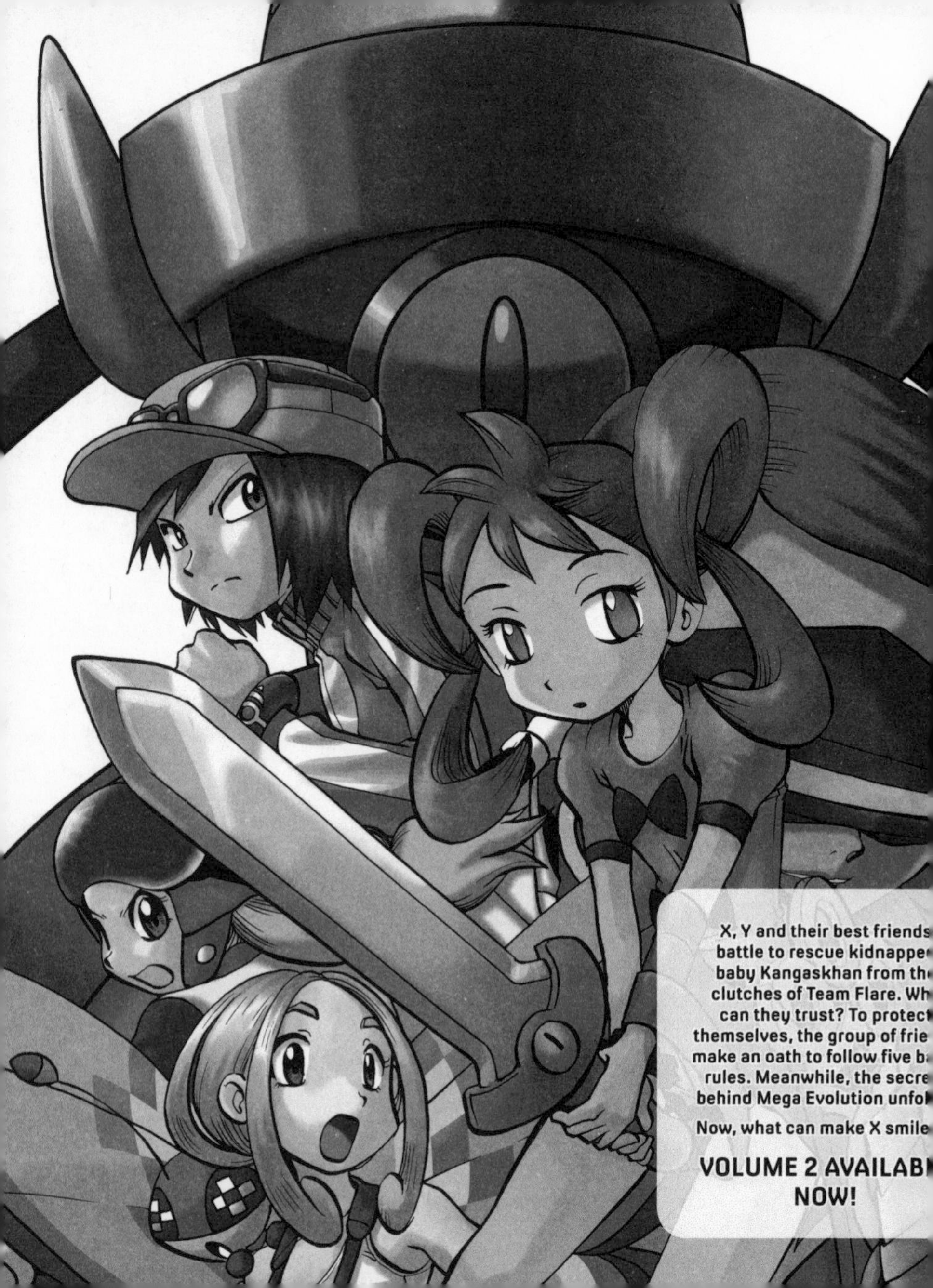
X, Y and their best friends
battle to rescue kidnappe
baby Kangaskhan from th
clutches of Team Flare. Wh
can they trust? To protect
themselves, the group of frie
make an oath to follow five b
rules. Meanwhile, the secre
behind Mega Evolution unfol
Now, what can make X smile
VOLUME 2 AVAILAB
NOW!

**Pokémon X • Y**
**Volume 1**
**Perfect Square Edition**

Story by HIDENORI KUSAKA
Art by SATOSHI YAMAMOTO

© 2014 The Pokémon Company International.
© 1995–2014 Nintendo / Creatures Inc. / GAME FREAK inc.
TM, ®, and character names are trademarks of Nintendo.
POCKET MONSTERS SPECIAL X·Y Vol. 1
by Hidenori KUSAKA, Satoshi YAMAMOTO
© 2014 Hidenori KUSAKA, Satoshi YAMAMOTO
All rights reserved.
Original Japanese edition published by SHOGAKUKAN.
English translation rights in the United States of America, Canada, the United Kingdom,
Ireland, Australia, New Zealand and India arranged with SHOGAKUKAN.

**English Adaptation**—Bryant Turnage
**Translation**—Tetsuichiro Miyaki
**Touch-up & Lettering**—Annaliese Christman
**Design**—Shawn Carrico
**Editor**—Annette Roman

Published by
VIZ Media, LLC
P.O. Box 77010
San Francisco, CA 94107

10 9 8 7 6 5 4
First printing, December 2014
Fourth printing, June 2017

  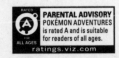

www.perfectsquare.com        www.viz.com

# The adventure continues in the Johto region!

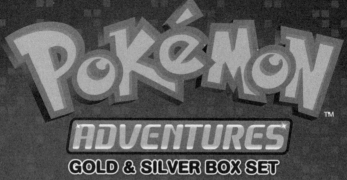

## POKÉMON ADVENTURES
### GOLD & SILVER BOX SET

Includes **POKÉMON ADVENTURES** Vols. 8-14 and a collectible poster!

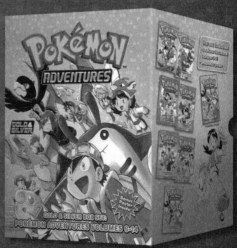

**Story by**
**HIDENORI KUSAKA**

**Art by**
**MATO,**
**SATOSHI YAMAMOTO**

More exciting Pokémon adventures starring Gold and his rival Silver! First someone steals Gold's backpack full of Poké Balls (and Pokémon!). Then someone steals Prof. Elm's Totodile. Can Gold catch the thief—or thieves?!

Keep an eye on Team Rocket, Gold... Could they be behind this crime wave?

VIZ media
www.viz.com

PERFECT SQUARE

RATED **A** FOR ALL AGES
ratings.viz.com

## Begin your Pokémon Adventure here in the Kanto region!

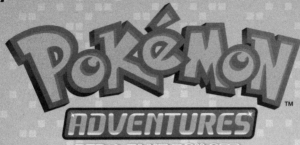

# POKÉMON™ ADVENTURES

### RED & BLUE BOX SET

*Story by* **HIDENORI KUSAKA** *Art by* **MATO**

Pokémon
Adventures
Bonus Poster Inside!
RED & BLUE BOX SET:
POKÉMON ADVENTURES VOLUMES 1-7

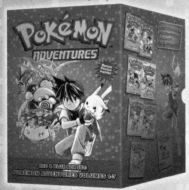

Includes **POKÉMON ADVENTURES** Vols. 1-7 and a collectible poster!

**All your favorite Pokémon game characters jump out of the screen into the pages of this action-packed manga!**

Red doesn't just want to train Pokémon, he wants to be their friend too. Bulbasaur and Poliwhirl seem game. But independent Pikachu won't be so easy to win over!

And watch out for Team Rocket, Red... They only want to be your enemy!

***Start the adventure today!***

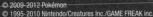

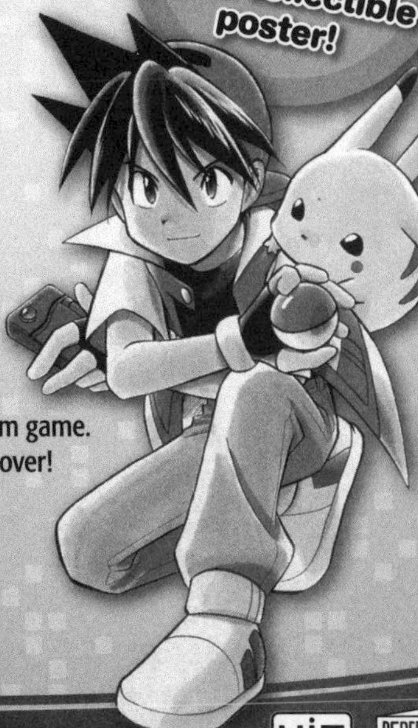

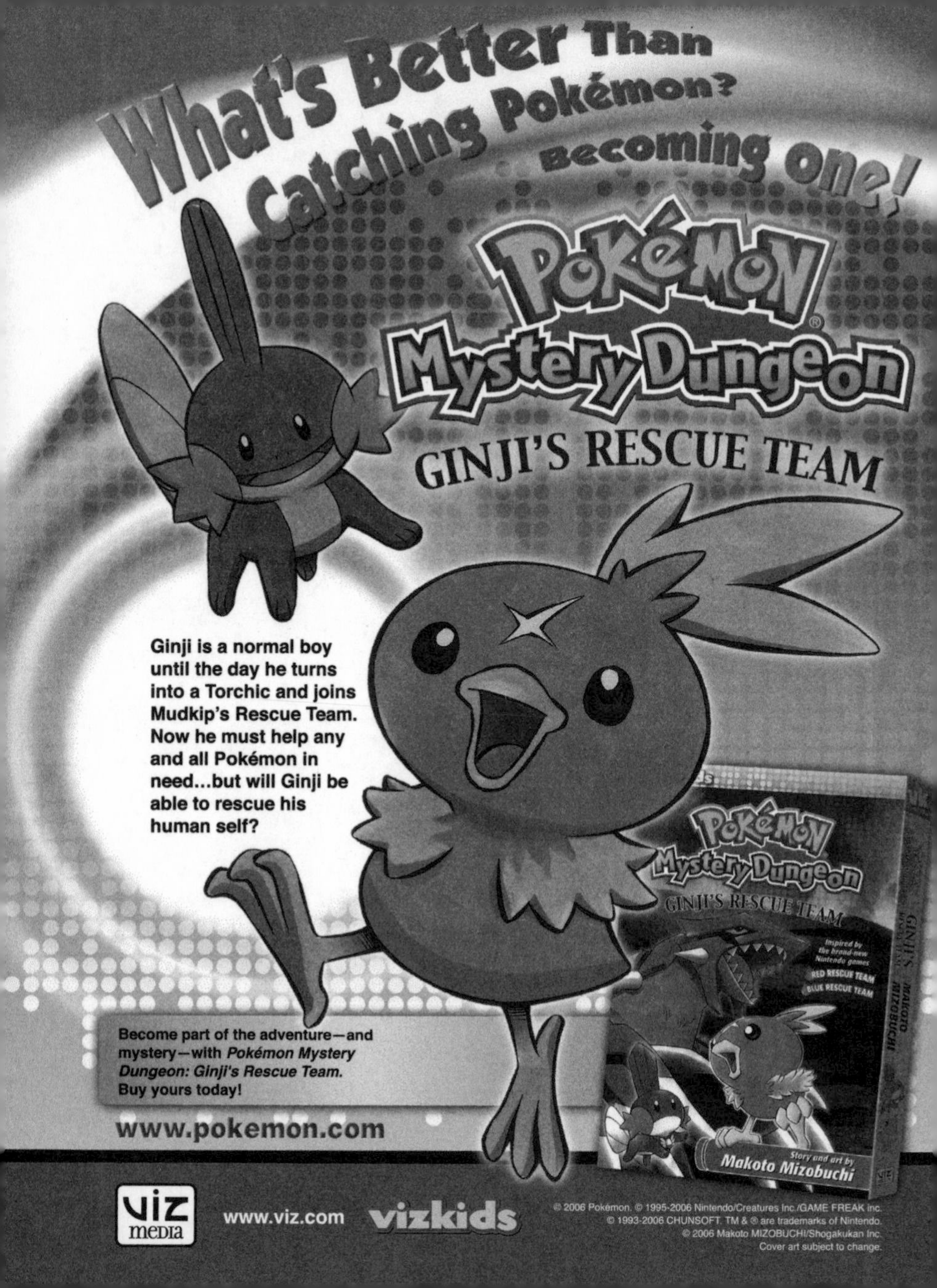
What's Better Than Catching Pokémon?
Becoming one!
POKÉMON®
Mystery Dungeon
GINJI'S RESCUE TEAM
Ginji is a normal boy until the day he turns into a Torchic and joins Mudkip's Rescue Team. Now he must help any and all Pokémon in need...but will Ginji be able to rescue his human self?
Become part of the adventure—and mystery—with Pokémon Mystery Dungeon: Ginji's Rescue Team. Buy yours today!
www.pokemon.com
POKÉMON Mystery Dungeon
GINJI'S RESCUE TEAM
Inspired by the brand-new Nintendo games
RED RESCUE TEAM
BLUE RESCUE TEAM
Story and art by
Makoto Mizobuchi
viz media
www.viz.com
vizkids
© 2006 Pokémon. © 1995-2006 Nintendo/Creatures Inc./GAME FREAK inc.
© 1993-2006 CHUNSOFT. TM & ® are trademarks of Nintendo.
© 2006 Makoto MIZOBUCHI/Shogakukan Inc.
Cover art subject to change.

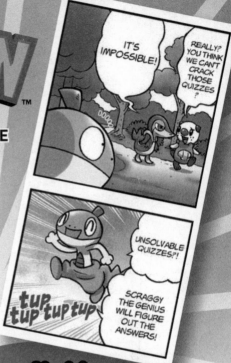
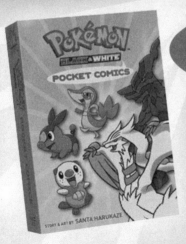

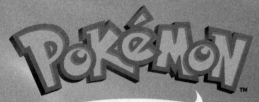
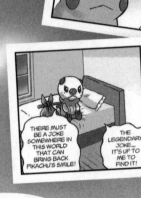

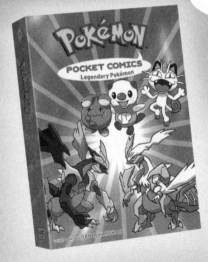
  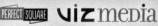

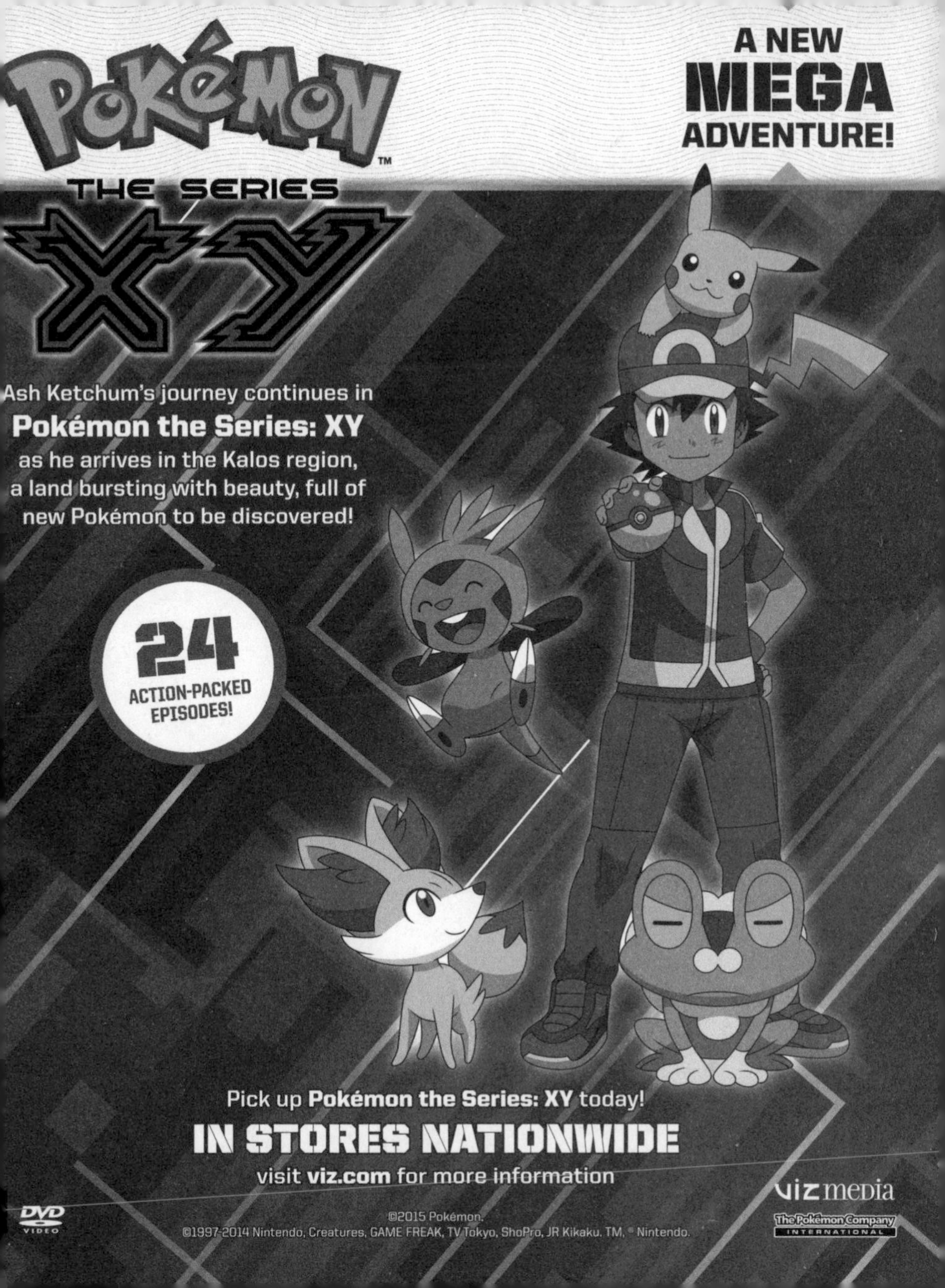
POKÉMON
THE SERIES
XY
A NEW
MEGA
ADVENTURE!
Ash Ketchum's journey continues in
Pokémon the Series: XY
as he arrives in the Kalos region,
a land bursting with beauty, full of
new Pokémon to be discovered!
24
ACTION-PACKED
EPISODES!
Pick up Pokémon the Series: XY today!
IN STORES NATIONWIDE
visit viz.com for more information
DVD VIDEO
viz media
The Pokémon Company INTERNATIONAL
©2015 Pokémon.
©1997-2014 Nintendo, Creatures, GAME FREAK, TV Tokyo, ShoPro, JR Kikaku. TM, ® Nintendo.

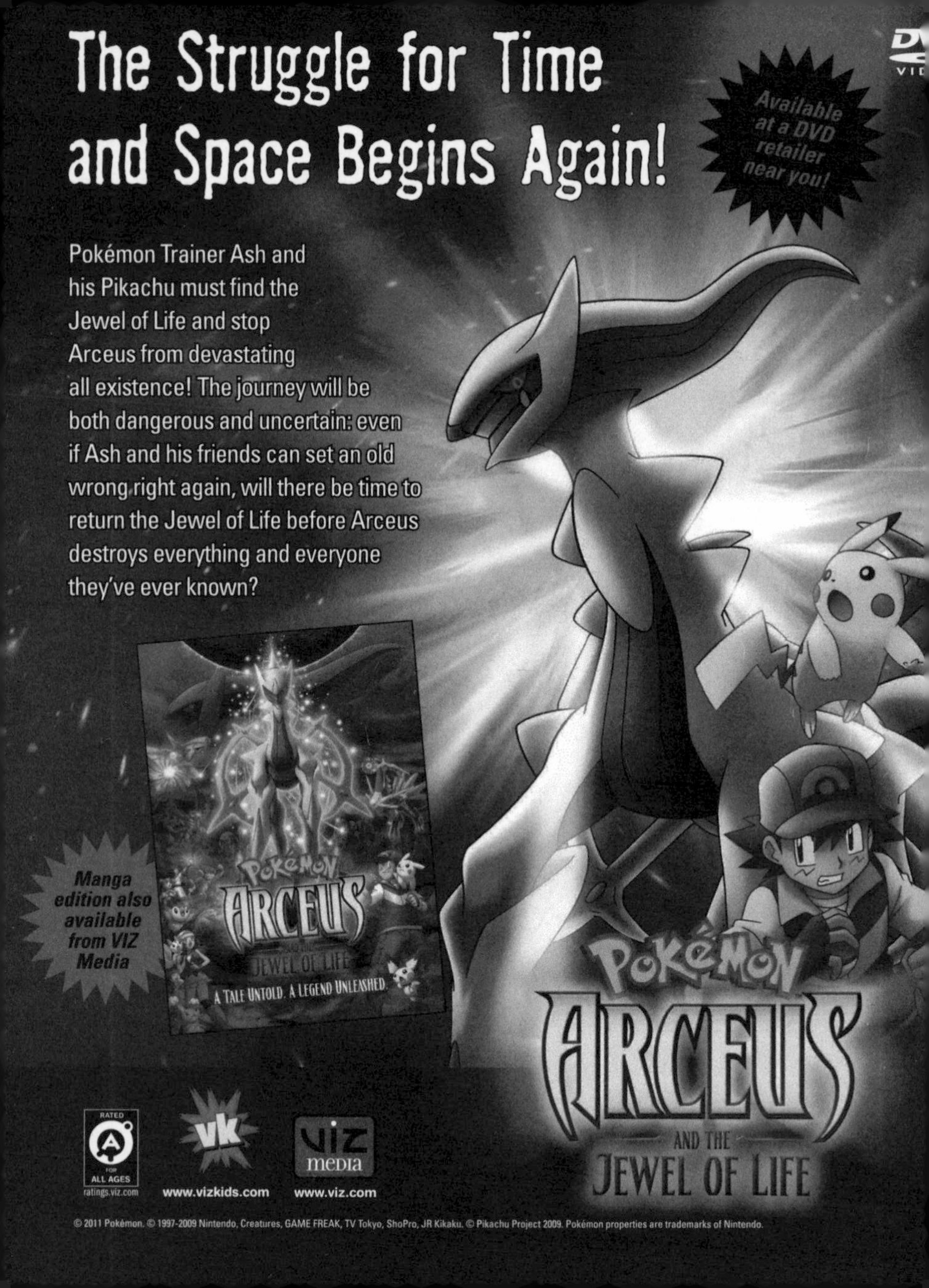
The Struggle for Time and Space Begins Again!
Available at a DVD retailer near you!
Pokémon Trainer Ash and his Pikachu must find the Jewel of Life and stop Arceus from devastating all existence! The journey will be both dangerous and uncertain: even if Ash and his friends can set an old wrong right again, will there be time to return the Jewel of Life before Arceus destroys everything and everyone they've ever known?
Pokémon
Arceus
and the
Jewel of Life
A Tale Untold. A Legend Unleashed.
Manga edition also available from VIZ Media
Pokémon
Arceus
and the
Jewel of Life
Rated A for All Ages
ratings.viz.com
vk
www.vizkids.com
VIZ media
www.viz.com
© 2011 Pokémon. © 1997-2009 Nintendo, Creatures, GAME FREAK, TV Tokyo, ShoPro, JR Kikaku. © Pikachu Project 2009. Pokémon properties are trademarks of Nintendo.

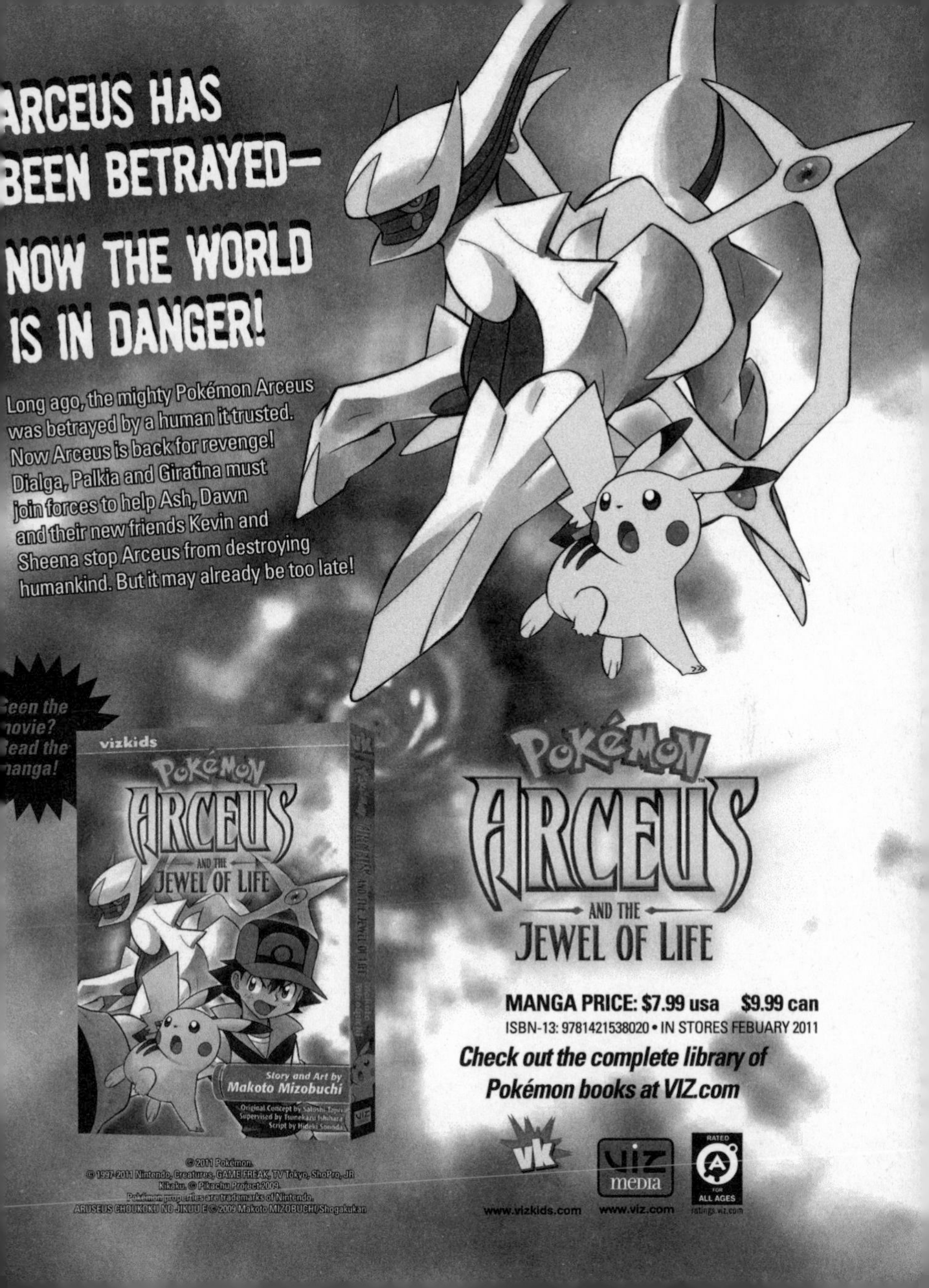

ARCEUS HAS BEEN BETRAYED—
NOW THE WORLD IS IN DANGER!
Long ago, the mighty Pokémon Arceus was betrayed by a human it trusted. Now Arceus is back for revenge! Dialga, Palkia and Giratina must join forces to help Ash, Dawn and their new friends Kevin and Sheena stop Arceus from destroying humankind. But it may already be too late!
een the
novie?
ead the
nanga!
vizkids
POKéMON
ARCEUS
AND THE
JEWEL OF LIFE
Story and Art by
Makoto Mizobuchi
Original Concept by Satoshi Tajiri
Supervised by Tsunekazu Ishihara
Script by Hideki Sonoda
POKéMON
ARCEUS
AND THE
JEWEL OF LIFE
MANGA PRICE: $7.99 usa $9.99 can
ISBN-13: 9781421538020 • IN STORES FEBUARY 2011
Check out the complete library of Pokémon books at VIZ.com
© 2011 Pokémon.
© 1997-2011 Nintendo, Creatures, GAME FREAK, TV Tokyo, ShoPro, JR Kikaku. © Pikachu Project 2009.
Pokémon properties are trademarks of Nintendo.
ARUSEUS CHOUKOKU NO JIKUU E © 2009 Makoto MIZOBUCHI/Shogakukan
vk
VIZ media
RATED
A
FOR
ALL AGES
www.vizkids.com
www.viz.com
ratings.viz.com

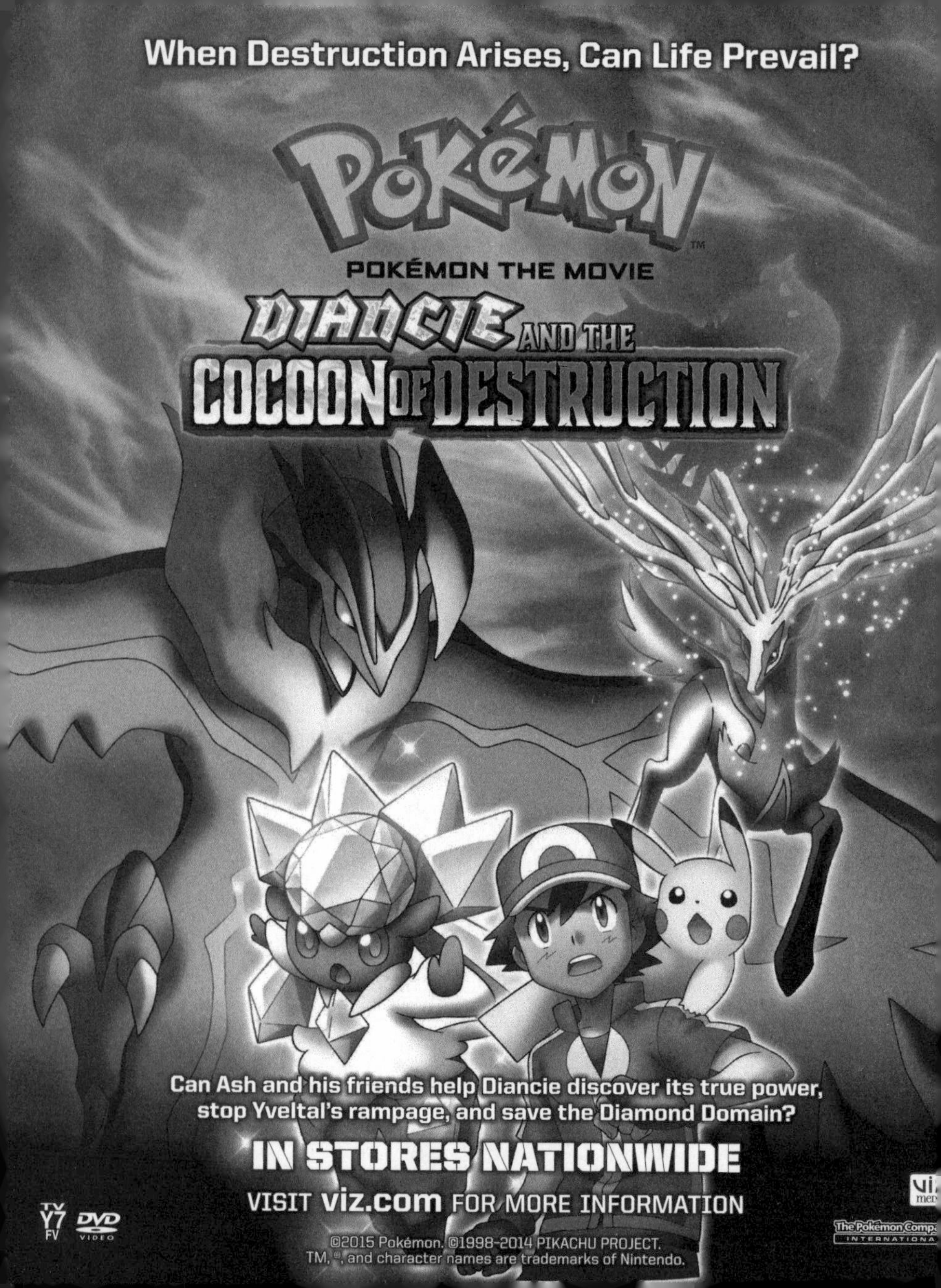
When Destruction Arises, Can Life Prevail?
POKÉMON
POKÉMON THE MOVIE
DIANCIE AND THE COCOON OF DESTRUCTION
Can Ash and his friends help Diancie discover its true power, stop Yveltal's rampage, and save the Diamond Domain?
IN STORES NATIONWIDE
VISIT viz.com FOR MORE INFORMATION
TV Y7 FV
DVD VIDEO
©2015 Pokémon. ©1998-2014 PIKACHU PROJECT.
TM, ®, and character names are trademarks of Nintendo.

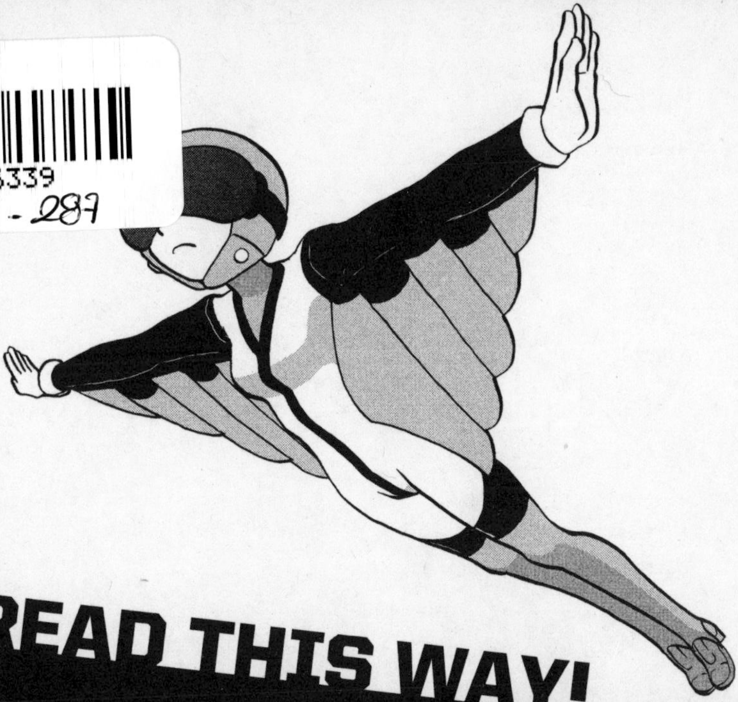

# <<< READ THIS WAY!

## THIS IS THE END OF THIS GRAPHIC NOVEL!

To properly enjoy this VIZ Media graphic novel, please turn it around and begin reading from right to left.

This book has been printed in the original Japanese format in order to preserve the orientation of the original artwork. Have fun with it!

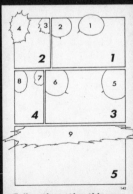

**Follow the action this way.**